David Goodis (1917–1967) is the author of *The Burglar, Dark Passage, Nightfall, Shoot the Piano Player* (all of which have been filmed), *The Blonde on the Street Corner, The Moon in the Gutter,* and *Of Tender Sin.*

Also by David Goodis and published by Serpent's Tail

The Moon in the Gutter
The Blonde on the Street Corner

OF TENDER SIN

David Goodis

Introduction by Adrian Wootton

Library of Congress Catalog Card Number: 00–102189

A complete catalogue record for this book can
be obtained from the British Library on request

The right of David Goodis to be identified as the author
of this work has been asserted by him in accordance
with the Copyright, Designs and Patents Act 1988

First published by Fawcett Publications, Inc., New York in 1952

First published in this edition in 2001 by Serpent's Tail,
4 Blackstock Mews, London N4 2BT

website: www.serpentstail.com

Printed in Great Britain by Mackays of Chatham, plc

10 9 8 7 6 5 4 3 2

Introduction by Adrian Wootton

American crime scribe, David Goodis (1917–1967), was the author of some of the most powerful pulp fiction novels to be published in the late 1940s/early 1950s. His work has also been adapted for several classic movies. Yet, as he once said – in typically self-deprecating terms, "I am no Raymond Chandler" and despite the efforts of fans, critics and filmmakers, his work has stubbornly remained a cult treat, resisting every attempt for wider recognition.

The man himself was also a shadowy figure, his relatively short life shrouded in mystery. The known facts, all rounded up in a solitary, still untranslated, French biography, are few and far between. Born in Philadelphia, he had a good, unspectacular education and, after university, plied his trade as an ad agency copywriter, whilst literally producing millions of words for pulp short story magazines and contributing scripts to radio serials. His big break and brief glimmer of fame came when his first crime novel, *Dark Passage*, was serialised in *The Saturday Evening Post*, a big American newspaper and, as a result, was bought by Warner Brothers to make into a Bogart and Bacall starring movie. Goodis also got a fat contract as a screenwriter out of the deal but, after a short-lived, unhappy marriage and a very few unsuccessful years in Tinseltown, he rapidly retreated back to his home town of Philadelphia. Living in the family home, almost entirely out of the public eye, David Goodis churned out one modestly successful paperback novel after another until a debilitating lawsuit against the producers of the TV show, *The Fugitive* (for allegedly plagiarising *Dark Passage*) precipitated his death in 1967.

In fact, aside from his relatively sedentary lifestyle, David Goodis's career followed a fairly typical path for a

crimewriter of that era. There are similarities between
himself and other notable writers, such as Jim Thompson.
But, unlike Thompson, the Goodis revival has never really
happened. Perhaps his work is too dark, too depressing
or just too plain sad to attract more than a small coterie
of readers.

To be absolutely fair, if it wasn't for French publishers
and French directors, Goodis's name may well have disappeared altogether in the 1960s and '70s. The importance
of the French Serie Noire crime imprint cannot be under-
estimated for many crime writers but particularly for
Goodis. It was through this that several of the greatest
French filmmakers of the last twenty-five years, including
Jean Luc Godard and François Truffaut, became aware of
Goodis and decided to adapt his work for the cinema.
Undoubtedly, the most famous of these was Truffaut's
classic film version of *Down There*, entitled *Tirez sur le
Pianiste* (*Shoot the Pianist*, 1960).

More recently, Jean-Jacques Beineix (the Director of
such international successes as *Diva* and *Betty Blue*) made
his own very expensive and controversial adaptation in
1983 of *Moon in the Gutter*, starring Gerard Depardieu and
Nastassia Kinski. Criminally under-rated at the time of
release, Beineix's film was not a box office success and so
once more Goodis failed to get the attention he deserved.

Whatever the whys and wherefores of Goodis's
obscurity, he is, undoubtedly, a damn fine writer; a unique
and distinctive talent whose best work stands alongside
anything else produced in the crime fiction genre. Goodis
does not tend to write about cops and robbers and he
never created a series character or detective that grew
from one book to the next. Instead, he mined a more
individual – albeit limited – seam of stories set in the back
streets, dumps and dives of urban any town in the USA
(although all his cities were really Philadelphia thinly
disguised).

David Goodis's characters occasionally are criminals but
this is not terribly important to him. The main thing for
Goodis is the emotional turmoil of life and people who,
for whatever reason, are losers – romantic, twisted,

sometimes exciting, but losers nonetheless, mired in circumstances from which there is no escape. The titles of his novels say it all – *Dark Passage, Of Missing Persons, Street of the Lost, Down There, Nightfall* and *The Moon in the Gutter.* His men are lonely, melancholic individuals, often artists who have cracked up or been in some way irreparably damaged. His women, on the other hand, veer from the plain, almost saintly sister/good girlfriend through to the sexually rapacious lover/whore. Whilst undoubtedly stereotypes, he invests them with such fierce life that you cannot help but get hooked. Goodis's world view may be despairing and depressing but his writing, replete with hardboiled dialogue and black humour, has – dare one say it – a poetic, almost frightening intensity that makes his stories compulsive page turners.

Of Tender Sin was published in March 1952, during David Goodis's most prolific and consistently successful publishing period. In fact, he generated no less than eight novels between 1951 and 1954. This novel followed the publication of *Cassidy's Girl*, the most popular book David Goodis ever wrote for the paperback market. Surprisingly, considering this, *Of Tender Sin* was not, as far as one can tell, a notable commercial hit and, as a result, it has remained one of his most obscure and least read novels. This, of itself, makes *Of Tender Sin* a fascinating curio but it is the content of the novel that singles it out in the Goodis canon and makes it particularly interesting for this re-publication.

On the face of it, *Of Tender Sin* has all the characteristics of a typical Goodis novel: Philadelphia set, a main character in the depths of psychological despair, brought on by sexual jealousy, a destructive/masochistic love affair, a criminal/low life milieu and the usual references to jazz and boxing. Admittedly, because of its focus on a particular individual, the novel lacks some of the depth of characterisation found in some of Goodis's very best work. Nevertheless, the book is unusually ambitious for Goodis because it is the only one of his novels that deals with drug abuse. Alcoholism features heavily in the Goodis oeuvre, probably because the author had his own

problems with the demon drink. *Of Tender Sin* still has
drunks in it but Goodis seems most concerned to explore
the low-rent drug dens of Philadelphia and there are very
good – if lurid – evocations of characters engaging in
heroin and cocaine abuse. In this way, *Of Tender Sin* is
reminiscent of – and possibly influenced by – Nelson
Algren's 1949 classic, *The Man with the Golden Arm,* and
indeed, could easily be described as Goodis's drug novel.
Perhaps this subject matter, very controversial for the time,
together with the distinct absence of a conventional
thriller plot goes some way to explaining its obscurity. It
is, therefore, even more welcome that we are now able to
re-read and re-appraise *Of Tender Sin* and see it for the,
maybe minor, but still challenging experiment it was in
Goodis's work.

Of Tender Sin was never adapted for the stage, cinema
or small screen. The last – and again, French – film adaptation of David Goodis's work, was nearly a decade ago
and, until the Serpent's Tail re-issue programme (also
including *The Moon in the Gutter* and *The Blonde on the Street
Corner*), there has been little or no publishing interest in
Goodis for over ten years. So, maybe this will finally spark
that long-lost revival or, at least, introduce him to a new
coterie of cult admirers to experience the particular
pleasures of Goodisville.

David Goodis's first and only non-crime novel was
called, somewhat appropriately, *Retreat from Oblivion* and,
thirty-three years on from his death, here's hoping.

OF TENDER SIN

Chapter 1

IT BEGAN WITH a shattered dream. The winter night was suddenly real and Alvin Darby was wide awake, seeing the darkness of the bedroom, the January whiteness beyond the window, then the wispy whiteness of the blanket that covered his wife in the adjoining twin bed. He took all that in to assure himself that he was truly awake. He lifted his fingers and applied pressure to his cheekbones, wanting to be doubly sure. But the contents of his mind did not seem to be wakeful thoughts. He had a feeling that someone uninvited had entered the house.

The house was a bungalow on the outskirts of Frankford, where Philadelphia gives way to the Roosevelt Boulevard. It was a neighborhood of new homes, low-priced but solidly constructed. The bungalows were detached and each had a reasonably wide skirting of lawn, a small garage, an open porch, and an altogether attractive appearance. They were nice little bungalows and it was a clean and pretty little neighborhood. But the fact remained that it was lower-middle-class, and Alvin Darby told himself it wouldn't sum up as the usual target of a burglar.

The term "burglar" echoed several times through his brain and he tried to smile derisively at himself. It was a situation he had seen many Sundays in the comic strips, wherein the wife thought she heard a noise somewhere in the house and the sleepy-eyed husband was forced to investigate, and usually it paid off with a laugh. But this time it wasn't the wife who had awakened. He looked at the other bed and saw Vivian sound asleep. Her dark hair was thick and soft and velvety, sweetly feminine and tender there against the pillow. He gazed at Vivian's dark hair and urged himself to enjoy the sight of it, to be thankful for Vivian and stop worrying about burglars. To stop being a damn fool and go back to sleep.

But now he was sitting up rigidly, and his eyes, focused on Vivian's dark hair, were no longer gazing, but set like stones, staring. It seemed to him that he had suddenly acquired another pair of eyes, planted in the back of his head, staring at something else. It was as though he could see beyond the bedroom wall, beyond the living room and through the hall leading toward a window through which a shape had entered.

It was a dark shape, much darker than the unlit space where it moved slowly, with a kind of calm furtiveness. He could see it coming very slowly, and he could sense the silent pressure of its tread on the soft carpets. He told himself it was coming toward the bedroom. The idea of a burglar had floated away, replaced by the idea of something less practical and certainly less realistic. Again he tried to smile at himself. Instead of building a smile, he gave way to a shiver.

As though he were steering a vehicle, Darby tugged at an imaginary wheel and steered his thoughts in a clearer direction. Of course all this wasn't actual, it was completely ridiculous. It was the kind of episode that might be suffered by a man who drank too much, or worried too much. He certainly wasn't in that category. Except for some beer now and then, he wasn't attracted to alcohol. And as far as worrying, he was in the unexciting yet nonetheless pleasant position of having no worries at all. The only problem he could think of was the fact that he had no problems.

At twenty-nine he had a healthy body and a brain that adjusted itself nicely to the demands of his daily work. He worked in the actuary department of a large insurance firm and earned the tidy take-home pay of eighty-five dollars a week. He owned a new Plymouth, and only last month he had made the final payment on the house. He wasn't indebted to anyone for as much as a thin dime. The cash in the bank was somewhere around eleven hundred dollars, and with eighty-five coming in every week, with the kind of job that put the accent on security, the financial picture was wholly satisfactory.

Darby moved the financial picture aside and tried to focus on something more personal. He was still tugging at the invisible steering wheel, but all at once it dissolved and became a liquid that became nothing. The feeling of nothingness began to climb and it went up very slowly along a stairway of musical sounds that he could hear distinctly even though he knew there was no sound. The soundless music went up and up and hit the higher octaves and became a soundless screaming as he sensed the approach of the dark shape moving through the house, moving toward him. Now he knew it was something serious. He recognized the fact that his awareness of a menace was increasing with each passing moment. If the feeling went on like this, if it continued just a little longer, it would become downright terror.

For God's sake. He said it without sound, but it was a shout inside himself. Don't sit here thinking about it. Get up and take a look around.

He thought he was moving off the bed, and realized with a sickening abruptness that he wasn't able to move. Then he was completely ashamed of himself, his masculine pride aimed anger at the fear. It was surely a prepos-

terous fear, and here he was coddling it, allowing it to
dominate him, actually to paralyze his physical being.
Better cut this off quick. And damn quick.

But he couldn't move. It gradually became a strangely
fascinating thing to acknowledge, the blunt truth that he
just couldn't move, he was immobilized. Fingers inside
his brain made another grab at the steering wheel, missed
it, tried again, missed again, tried frantically and caught
the steering wheel and held on. Then very slowly he
steered his thoughts away from the fear as he said to himself, It doesn't make sense. There's no reason for it. Not
a single shred of a reason.

He was looking at Vivian. Still sound asleep, she had
turned on her side, so that now he could see her face. She
had an adorable face, and it was lit now with the glow of
the winter moon pouring in to bounce off a mirror and
come back and settle gently on her bed. Under the blanket
the outline of her body was slender and displayed a certain innocence, a precious quality far more significant
than the elegance of her form. She seemed to radiate kind-
ness and essential goodness, and Darby, trying to measure
the value of her, told himself it was immeasurable.

"There's a prize." He said it in a whisper. "There's a
real prize." He felt the gentle throbbing of a limitless affection. Sound asleep there, like a child. Getting on
toward twenty-four, but she looked about nineteen. She
had been nineteen when he married her. Well, she would
always be nineteen. Always a treasure. He leaned across
the bed, trying to kiss her with his eyes.

But then he saw that her sleep was not calm. He saw
the troubled frown. And something else that caused him
to turn his head away, wondering if he had really seen it.

It had to do with the color of her hair. He was certain
that her hair had suddenly changed color from dark
brown to a pale silver yellow.

Impossible, of course, and so he blinked several times,
telling his eyes to behave. And then he looked again. And
this time he saw the velvety dark hair.

He decided that the moonlight had been playing a
trick. Just an optical illusion. And yet, even as he accept-

ed this as a fact, he gave way to a fervent wish that her hair would actually change to that other color, that pale silver yellow.

It was a crazy sort of thinking, and he tried, with all his mental might, to figure it out.

Then, within the increasing chaos that swirled through his brain, an incredible force went into action and took his thoughts away from Vivian, away from this house, away from present time.

He saw a different house, a different year. Saw it clearly, in detail, the little house in the old neighborhood, down around Fourth and Green. When he was twelve years old, and his parents were visiting some neighbors down the street, and he was alone in the house with his sister Marjorie. They were in the parlor, listening to the radio. But he was paying scarcely any attention to the program. He was looking at Marjorie. She was so nice to look at. There were a lot of pretty fifteen-year-old girls around Fourth and Green, but his sister Marjorie was the prettiest. And the sweetest, and the nicest. She always spoke so softly, so gently. When she was in a room, it became a garden. When she turned the corner of Green Street and came walking down Fourth, it was always the approach of a princess. And here, in the parlor, with Guy Lombardo on the radio, the princess held court in her garden while the royal musicians made wonderful music. And she lifted one hand and waved it from side to side in time with the melody, as the fingers of her other hand drifted idly through her silver-yellow hair.

Darby shut his eyes tightly. He gripped his wrist, applied pressure as though trying to stop the flow of blood from a cut.

"Good God," he gasped. "What's happening here? What's all this with silver-yellow hair?"

Telling himself that Marjorie's hair hadn't been that color.

Couldn't be. Of course not. His sister's hair had been dark brown, very dark.

Really? he asked himself without sound. You sure about that?

He wasn't sure. He sat there in the bed, motionless, yet with the frantic knowledge that he was in the midst of some terrific struggle. Trying to remember the color of Marjorie's hair. Unable to remember.

Then he heard his own hissed whisper. "God damn it."

Because it went back and forth, back and forth. One moment Marjorie's hair was dark brown, the next it was silver yellow. Then dark again. Then silver yellow.

The hell with this. Once more he spoke without sound. What difference does it make? What do I care what color her hair was?

But he knew that he did care. Knew it was terribly important.

For some weird but completely unknown reason.

At that point, he managed to laugh at himself. He told himself he was making a big thing out of nothing. Chances were, all this was due to a bad tooth or an upset stomach. Maybe it was that tangerine he had eaten just before going to bed.

But no. His teeth were in perfect condition. And tangerines agreed with him, no matter when he ate them.

All right, then. maybe it was the result of something rotten that had happened during the day.

But then, as he recalled the events of the day, he realized that nothing rotten had happened. Unless it was the weather. The winter weather in Philadelphia was always miserable. He told himself to start thinking about the weather. Or any kind of external thing that had nothing to do with himself. Like the fire engines he had seen whizzing down Sixth Street during his lunch hour. The hunchback in the Frankford elevated, selling newspapers and glaring at his customers as though they were enemies. The seven-foot giant sandwiched between advertising signs stating that Max the Clothier fitted all sizes. And an immaculately dressed drunk, politely ejected from a midtown bar. And a platinum blonde who didn't look where she was going and bumped into a shipping clerk, who dropped his packages and gazed wearily at the sky.

It had been a day like any other day. His work at the

insurance office had cruised along smoothly and he had
come home to a pleasant dinner with a pleasant wife. He
had watched a fight between fast featherweights, telecast
from New York, and had followed Vivian into the bedroom at a few minutes past eleven. She had seemed to be
asleep immediately and he sat up in bed for a while,
slowly turning the pages of a photo magazine. And that
was it. That was the day.

All right, then, maybe something had happened yesterday. Or the day before that. Maybe last week or last
month. He shifted into reverse gear and started to go back
and couldn't find anything. It was like retracing a journey
across a lake on which there were no ripples. There were
scarcely any changes through the weeks and months and
two years and three years. The only disturbing issues were
the issues he read in the newspapers. Since his marriage
to Vivian four years ago, his life had been uneventful and
typical except for the fact that he was never bored with
Vivian. Never annoyed or restless, like the typical hus-
bands he knew. Vivian possessed just the right blending
of vivacity and composure, knew when to ask questions
and what questions to ask. And most important, the
quality that made her a blue-ribbon wife, she knew when
to leave him the hell alone.

He was feeling better now. He told himself he felt a lot
better. The trouble had come and gone, just one of those
inexplainable spells that could happen to anyone. The
thing to do was forget about it and go back to sleep. He
lowered his head toward the pillow, and just as he
touched the pillow he was seized with the feeling that
someone was in the hall outside the bedroom door.

Then it was like a big bubble bursting inside him, and
as it fell apart he was able to move. He rolled himself off
the bed, slipped into his bathrobe and slippers, and
moved toward the door. It didn't occur to him that he
ought to have some sort of weapon, but as he neared the
dressing table and saw himself in the moonlit mirror he
sensed that he was defenseless.

For an instant he hesitated there before the mirror,
staring at himself. He saw his wide eyes and something

that was beyond the eyes. He didn't see the physical structure of his medium-sized body, didn't see the straw-color hair, the average ears and nose, the average good looks. He was seeing someone who was being hurled far and far away from the area of average or typical or whatever they wanted to call it. The unknown party outside the bedroom door was inviting him to come on out and say hello, then come along down an unlit road, a very long road. Where there was nothing on either side, there was nothing at all, just the road going down and down.

He opened the door and stepped into the hall. The hall light was on and the hall was empty. In the living-room he switched on a lamp, looked and listened, and there wasn't anything but the walls and furniture. Then the bathroom, then the hall again, then down the hall and through the breakfast nook and into the kitchen. He stood in the kitchen with his fingers probing the bathrobe pockets for cigarettes and not finding any. He wished there were some liquor in the house. It was probably true what they said about liquor, that it helped a lot at moments like this.

Maybe a glass of cold water would do the trick. What he really needed, he decided angrily, was a bucket of ice-cold water splashed full in his face. Or a hefty kick in the rear. He took the water jar from the refrigerator, filled a glass, and was lifting it to his lips when he heard the footsteps and knew she was coming toward the kitchen.

It was like cowering at the base of an icy mountain and seeing the approaching avalanche. He begged himself to realize it was only his wife, this was only a kitchen, it was just a night in January in the city of Philadelphia, and a man named Darby had climbed out of bed to get a drink of water. That was all. And his tongue tasted blood as panic caused him to bite deeply at the side of his mouth.

Then Vivian came into the kitchen, adjusting the belt of her robe. Her eyes and lips were somewhere between a smile and a frown as she watched him drinking the water. He looked at her, tried to smile past the edge of the glass, and felt the water trickling down his chin.

"You're spilling it," Vivian said.

He put the glass on the sink. "I'm half asleep."

Vivian inclined her head just a little, studying him. The smile began to fade. The frown stayed where it was. She didn't say anything.

For no special reason, he picked up the glass, looked at it as though it meant something, put it down again. He opened his mouth to speak, but the words sailed away from his reach and he found himself staring at Vivian just as if all the trouble were over on her side of the room.

Her voice was calm. "What woke you up?"

He shrugged. "I thought I heard something." He tried a laugh, but it was a dry grinding sound, more like choking. "Thought it was a burglar."

"You serious?"

He didn't like the way she said that. His eyes were sullen. "It's possible, isn't it? This house is no different from any other house. No house is burglarproof."

"You don't have to get angry."

"I'm not angry."

Vivian backed to the doorway. She turned her head and threw a quick look toward the hall and the living room. It seemed she did it only to humor him, tolerating his foolish notion of a burglar. And she said, "Could have been a mouse."

"I didn't know we had mice."

"We don't," she murmured. "But it's always best to make sure. I'll set a trap tomorrow."

He shrugged again. "All right, do that. Now let's go back to sleep."

He thought that would end it. He started toward the doorway. But Vivian blocked it, standing there. Just looking at him. The floor of the kitchen became a chessboard and she seemed to be waiting for his next move.

It couldn't be handled with words, he knew. And he couldn't very well shove her aside.

"What's bothering you?" she asked.

"Nothing."

"You sure?"

He nodded. But he realized he'd have to do better

than that. He came toward her with the idea of giving
her a kiss. Her lips were made just right for kissing, and
as he moved closer he saw a warm-blooded woman with
an adorable face and an exquisite body and it shouldn't
be at all difficult to put his arms around her and taste
her lips.

Then all at once he stopped and winced, and a quiver
wriggled its way through his brain. The thought of kissing her was horrible, like touching something grotesque
and slimy.

To make things worse, he saw that she wanted him to
kiss her. The hot glow was in her eyes, and she was breathing deeply so that her breasts swelled and beckoned, telling him it would be nice and pleasant. and all he had to
do was just come a step closer.

He stepped back, glaring at her as though she were
some sort of temptress and not the woman to whom he
had been married for four years.

"God damn it," he muttered. "What's going on here?"

Vivian said nothing. She lifted her shoulder a little
and gazed at him through half-closed eyes and he saw the
long eyelashes and the allure.

He felt angry with her.

His voice was thick. "You look like you want it bad."

Her lips scarcely moved. "Would that be so strange?"

"Real bad, Vivian?"

She had a hand on her smoothly rounded hip. Letting
the hand move around in lazy little circles that fondled
the roundness. "I'm not playing," she murmured.

That thrilled him, and he didn't want to be thrilled.
He wanted to be sullen. "What do you want me to do, put
you down on the floor? Right here in the kitchen?"

"The kitchen." Her eyes were languid, gazing at the
linoleum floor. "Well, we've done it in the living room.
In the hall. In every other room in the house. So why not
the kitchen?"

He tried to get rid of the thick heat in his throat.
"You'd get a kick out of that, wouldn't you?"

"Listen," she said, "the way I feel now, I'd go up on the
roof with you, stark naked."

His lips tightened. "Don't talk like that. I don't like it when you talk that way."

"Really?" Her eyes remained languid, her voice quiet and creamy. "You're beginning to sound like a Sunday-school teacher."

He stood there stiffly. He said, "I'm your husband."

"Then let me know it."

He stared at the floor. The floor was like a blank sheet of paper.

"Come on," Vivian said.

He pulled his eyes away from the floor and scowled at her. "Say, what the hell's wrong with you tonight?"

Her smile came slowly and easily. "Nothing to worry about. I hope it will always be that way for me."

"Is that so? I thought winter was the cold season."

She said, "The season of the year has nothing to do with it."

He had a feeling that he was being pushed into a corner. He wondered what to say. Finally he said, "You look very nice, you know? I like the way you're built. You're really built."

"Thank you." But she seemed to know he had said it just to say something. Her eyes narrowed just a little. There was a moment of silent fencing. Then she threw away her blade and the moment ended with her voice sirupy and steamy, with all the wanting in it, saying, "But I don't want to stand here talking about it."

It came at him slowly. But the impact was hard. And before he could check the unreasonable reply, he heard himself growling, "God damn it, cut it out. You sound like a tramp."

She winced. But that was all. In the next instant the lazy smile was there again, and she murmured, "I've often wondered about that."

The growl remained in his throat. "About what?"

"What it would be like. To be a tramp."

The growl rose again, but he swallowed it. And then he said, more calmly," I guess I *am* a bit upset. And I wish you'd calm down."

"I don't want to calm down," she told him. She leaned

her elbow against the wall and kept the other hand on her hip. "Can't you understand?"

"Shut up," he cut in loudly. "Shut up."

She didn't seem to hear. "Tell me," she said. "Tell me the truth about something, will you?"

"What do you mean?"

Without raising her voice, "I think you know what I mean."

All he could do was go on blinking at her and shaking his head slowly.

She took her elbow away from the wall. Her hand slid away from her hip. She was bent forward. It was a startlingly sudden change, every trace of restraint pushed aside, giving way to the fury. Her eyes glittered dangerously.

Her voice jabbed at him. "Tell me the truth. Have you been running around?"

He met her with his own anger. "I won't answer that." The anger flared, and he took a step toward her. "That's what I call a cheap, lousy question."

"You'll answer it anyway." She stepped back, not in retreat, but in order to block the doorway. She was breathing hard. Her face was flushed and her arms were quivering bars that dared him to shove her away from the doorway.

He felt the tenseness of his jaw muscles. "All right," he said. "The answer is no. I haven't been running around." And after it was out, the anger went away and there was no tenseness and he was able to smile dimly, to say, "Now it's my turn to ask a question. What's the big idea? What put a thing like that in your mind?"

She continued to block the doorway. Her eyes were set hard, studying him. Not saying anything.

"Well?" he demanded.

But still she didn't say anything. She just went on studying him, her head slanted, as though she was seeing something she couldn't quite figure out.

Then finally she wet her lips, as though the words needed lubrication in order to come out.

And she said, "It's been weeks now."

It was a sledge hammer, and he heard a dazed voice that couldn't possibly be his own. "What? What's that?"

"You heard me. I said weeks."

And then, not moving from where he stood, but with a feeling that he was staggering around in circles, "How many weeks?"

"You really don't know?"

His fingers pressed against his temple. "I can't remember."

"Well, then," she said, "if you're really interested, it's been three weeks and a day."

The sledge hammer hit him again. He realized that his memory of these past few weeks, as far as Vivian was concerned, was more or less of a blank.

He was able to admit to himself that he couldn't understand it. Before, all she had to do was look at him in a certain way and he'd be feverish with wanting her. Perhaps, during these recent weeks, she hadn't looked at him in that certain way. He tried to recall.

And he couldn't recall.

It was like holding a commuter's ticket to nowhere and making a nightly excursion even though he was right there in the same room with her, night after night.

But damn it, the fault couldn't be all on his side. It surely couldn't be that he was physically incapable.

Or maybe he was.

Maybe it was true what they said in certain books. That no man escapes it. That it happens because sooner or later it's bound to happen. Something on the order of a batting slump. The power just goes away and then after a while it comes back. Or never comes back.

But no. It couldn't be happening to him. Why, for God's sake, there was no reason for it. No reason at all. After all, he was young, he was in perfect health. It just couldn't be that he had lost his need for her soft lips and the thrusting delight of her breasts and the sweet hot satin of her thighs. The thought of living in this house with Vivian and not wanting her was an utterly impossible thought.

And yet it was bluntly true. Three weeks and a day.

He heard Vivian saying, "For you and me, three weeks is a long time, don't you think?" Giving it to him gently, as she turned to walk out of the kitchen. And then, just before she walked out, she flashed him the look. The look that said, It's all right, honey, and I'm not sore about anything, and if you want me I'll be in the bedroom.

So then he was alone with himself in the kitchen, staring at the empty doorway that led to the hall that led to the bedroom. He took a step toward the doorway and stopped and realized he was afraid to go into the bedroom.

What he had to do, he told himself, was to think in terms of wanting to do it, instead of not wanting to do it. After all, it came under the heading of pleasure. And there was no greater pleasure. Especially with this dark-eyed, dark-haired girl, this ultimate of prizes who made them all look twice whenever she came walking down the street.

He told himself he'd really give her a time tonight. He'd make up for all these past weeks.

He went out of the kitchen and down the hall and into the bedroom.

Between the twin beds the table lamp was lit and Vivian was sitting up in bed, her hands clasped around her knees. Her lustrous dark hair flowed thickly, luxuriantly, across her bared shoulders, and the low cut of her nightgown revealed the eager fullness of her breasts. She was giving him the look. No smile, just the look.

Then, as he came toward her bed, she rolled the double blanket down and away and he saw the full delight of her body under the flimsy fabric of her nightgown. He climbed into the bed beside her, and even before he touched her it seemed that he could feel the heat coming from the racing blood and the trembling flesh.

He kissed her and felt her arms straining around his middle. He kissed her again and became dizzy as she returned his kiss with a burning frenzy. He tasted the intoxicating nectar of her mouth, and went on kissing her while his hands came against firm breasts, while she writhed and squirmed and made the little animal sounds that never failed to drive him wild with hunger for her.

So that now, very quickly, he was hungry for her and he had the right feeling, the knowledge of readiness. His eyes were closed and he could feel the pressure of her limbs as she silently told him: Now.

Just then he opened his eyes and saw her parted lips. And his eyes traveled upward past her exquisitely shaped nose and her smooth brow and up to her dark hair.

He stared at Vivian's dark hair.

Wishing it wasn't dark. Wishing it was silver yellow.

And knowing, in that instant, he wouldn't be able to go through with it.

He pulled himself away and sat on the edge of the bed and looked at the floor.

He heard Vivian saying, "What happened?"

"I don't know."

He felt her hand on his shoulder as she said, "Listen, honey. Listen to me—"

"For God's sake!" He leaped up to get away from her touch. He walked to the window, turned, and crossed the room and recrossed it, not looking at her. Finally he climbed into his own bed.

"Come back here," Vivian said. It was quiet pleading.

He pushed his face deep into the pillow. His eyes were shut tightly. "Do me a favor," he groaned. "Just leave me alone. Let me go to sleep."

"You won't sleep," she said. "Neither will I."

He opened his eyes and saw Vivian getting out of bed. He watched her while she put on her robe and walked back and forth. Her head was bent low and for a moment he thought she was crying. But then, as she passed near his bed, he saw that she was gazing thoughtfully at the floor, like someone trying to solve a puzzle.

Presently she looked at him and said, "You know, I may be conceited, but I just can't believe you don't want me any more."

"Don't talk like that," he told her. "You know that isn't it."

"Then what is it?" she challenged.

He struggled to find an adequate reply. Finally he

said, "I'm just tired, that's all. I've been working hard."
It sounded more or less adequate, so he went on, "They're
rushing us to death down at the office. I've been knocking
myself out."

She moved toward him. Her smile was gentle scolding.
"Why didn't you tell me before?"

He shrugged, getting it across smoothly but hating himself for the lie. "Didn't want to worry you."

Vivian patted his shoulder and said, "I'm sorry, honey.
But really, you should have told me." She leaned down
and her lips brushed his forehead. "Don't let it bother
you. Forget about tonight. There are other nights."

He saw her backing away from the bed and then walking toward the door, and he said, "Where are you going?"

Casually, "That burglar business. Maybe you really
heard something. I'm calling the police."

He sat up, frowning. "You serious? They'll keep us up
all night."

"No, they won't," Vivian said. "I'll just tell them we
thought we heard a noise and we want to be on the safe
side. All they'll do is ride around the block and make a
checkup."

He gestured indifferently. Suddenly he was very tired.
He lowered his head to the pillow and heard the door
closing. The sound gave him a deep feeling of calm and
security. It was like the special winter nights of his child-
hood, the very cold nights when his sister Marjorie came
in to make sure he was safely tucked in under the quilt,
and smiled at him and said good night and gently closed
the door.

Then sometimes there would be a really pleasant treat.
For Marjorie would sit on the edge of the bed and talk to
him for a little while. And tell him a bedtime story, or
describe something funny that had happened in school
that day. It was so nice to rest there under the warm quilt
and listen to the soft, creamy voice of Marjorie. To look
up and see her smiling face, like a white flower glowing in
the darkness of the room. And the special luster of her
pale green eyes. And the glimmering treasure of her
silver-yellow hair.

Darby stiffened. His hands became fists and he pressed them hard against his forehead. Pleading with himself to recall correctly whether Marjorie's hair had been dark brown or silver yellow.

He opened his eyes. Something caused him to sit up. And lift himself out of the bed. Something caused him to move slowly across the floor, and for a quivering moment he wondered what it was. Then, as he slowly and quietly opened the door, he didn't care what it was. Knew only that he mustn't make a sound.

The light came from the breakfast nook, where Vivian was talking on the phone. He worked his way carefully toward the breakfast nook and heard what she was saying and knew almost immediately that she wasn't talking to the police.

Chapter 2

WHAT SURPRISED HIM MOST was the fact that he wasn't at all surprised. He knew, just as sure as he was alive, that he hadn't expected anything else but this. There was no particular reason why he should have expected it, and now, as he heard it and knew it was happening, he understood what they meant when they claimed there were some things that couldn't be explained.

He stood there in the darkness of the hall outside the breakfast room and heard her saying, "Can't you see me tomorrow?" and then a long pause. And then, "But I've got to see you. Can't you understand?" A longer pause. He heard her hurried breathing. "Of course, darling, I know that, but . . ." A tapping sound, her fingertips nervous on the tabletop. "No, don't say that. Please don't. He mustn't find out."

Darby was smiling, he didn't know the smile was there, but his lips played with it as he started backward very slowly, with the same quiet he had used in his approach. It became a frozen smile as he arrived in the bedroom, making no sound at all as he climbed back into bed. He arranged himself comfortably under the blanket and closed his eyes. He breathed deeply, the deep and heavy rhythm of sleep. When he heard the door opening, he knew she was looking at him to make sure he was asleep. Chances were she was biting her lower lip, the way she always did when anything bothered her. He listened with a kind of enjoyment as her footsteps moved across the room toward her bed. Then the darkness under his eyelids became darker as the lamp was switched off.

Well, he thought mildly, knowing the mildness was only a breeze riding in front of a raging storm. Well, this is very interesting.

22

It was especially interesting because not once in all the four years of their marriage had he questioned her fidelity. It was something he had taken completely for granted. Just like knowing, when he went to sleep each night, that he would wake up in the morning. He had never seen her give so much as a second look at another man, and even if she had, he would have thought nothing of it. He had seen a good many men looking at her with admiration, but it never worried him, never angered him. He couldn't very well blame the men, because she was really something to look at. There were times when he'd seen her coming down the street and he'd forget that it was his wife and say to himself, Now, there's a nice number, that's really nice. Then as she'd come closer it was like saying hello to someone inside himself, someone who would never go away.

Now he was starting to feel the full force of the shock. It was a strange shock, because it didn't hit him all at once, with one big blast. It came like big rollers moving slowly toward a beach. With the same deliberateness, shoving everything else aside and coming in slow and hard and heavy. Then with the crashing sound, the angry foam, the insane fury as he realized how he had been deceived and betrayed.

It must have been going on for a long time. Her voice, speaking into the phone, had contained something deeper than intimacy, as though she had known the man for years and years. And yet, just a little while ago, standing there in the kitchen, she had said, "It's been weeks now." So now he knew, in all the other countless weeks when he had crossed over from his bed to hers, the face and body that waited for him was just a rotten fake.

He must have sensed it weeks ago, sensed some change in her mood, some vague change, but sufficiently significant to strangle the cords of his desire. It could happen like that, one little thing leading to another, a lot of little things collecting there and growing like the germs of a plague. Until it really hit and exploded, just like the explosion tonight.

A burglar. Well, he hadn't been far off. In a sense, it

was a burglary, and yet that was putting it lightly. The factor that made it unbearable was the value he had placed on her, the degree of unity that had made it impossible for him to gaze at any other woman with more than objective appraisal.

His eyes were open now and he looked up and saw the black ceiling and wished it would give way and come down to crush both her and himself. At least there'd be some truth in that. There wasn't any truth in this, the two beds side by side, the married couple who breathed the same air in the same room while a third person waited somewhere for the next convenient hour.

A third person. Someone she had known for a long time. Then it must be someone he knew. His mind began to print the names of men with whom they were both acquainted. Going far back to the days when he was courting her and they went to a lot of parties and had a lot of friends. The summers in Wildwood and the gang toasting marshmallows on the beach. Good old George and Sam and Johnny. And Steve and Ralph and Charley. And Frank and Pete and Bob. On and on like that, too many names, too many possibilities. But wait. Hold it. Try Pete again. Stay with Pete.

Pete Lanson. The snappy dresser, the smooth dancer, the life of the party. Pete had featured a mustache in high school, had been the first of the crowd to own a hopped-up jalopy. At twenty-five, Pete was a crackerjack door-to-door salesman, selling refrigerators as though they were nickel candy. At least, that was what Pete claimed, despite the fact that he was always borrowing money. He was liked by everyone, even his creditors, who couldn't help smiling weakly as he gave them the old excuses. After all, he was such a nice guy, and when he did have it he was big with it, he insisted on picking up the check.

And the girls, they swarmed all over Pete. He had the natural smile, the dashing good looks. Somewhat on the tall side, very lean, and always shaved and spruced up, always poised and displaying an effortless charm that instantly put him in the spotlight. Too many girls were wild about him, so he never had a steady girl friend. But

he was always with a girl. It was amazing the way he
avoided becoming involved. He eased in and out of situations like a smiling, good-natured eel, and with disarming
honesty he confessed to each girl that he was a reckless
devil who mustn't be taken seriously. Of course, they went
for that, most of them, and generally Pete had no problem
getting in and no difficulties when he made his friendly
exit.

Yet now the memory that smashed at Darby was a
particular scene wherein Pete had considerable trouble
saying good-by. The scene was vivid at this moment and
Darby was staggered not only by its vividness, but more
by the fact that long ago he had erased it from his mind.
He had erased it on the same night it had happened. His
wedding night.

He wore a tuxedo, and Vivian was entrancing in white.
Against a wall of yellow birds and flowers there was the
dark oak of a grandfather clock, and the lace-covered
buffet table. There were heaped dishes and gleaming
silverware and everything was in order. It was the house
in West Philadelphia where Vivian's folks lived. The
guests were starting to arrive and then the party was
started, the bottles were opened, the kisses exchanged, the
greetings loud and happy.

The groom, surrounded by well-wishers, smilingly ex-
cused himself and went searching for his bride. There
was a hallway, sort of dark because the lamps were old-
fashioned and didn't give much of a glow. A door was
open and he heard Vivian's voice. He was about to enter
the room when he heard the voice of Pete Lanson.

"I'm sorry," Pete was saying.

"That helps a lot, doesn't it?" Her tone was bitter.

"I'm really sorry, honest I am." Pete sounded very serious, and that was unusual. The bridegroom stood outside
the door and wondered what the hell was going on.

Then Vivian's voice. "When are you leaving?"

"Tonight."

"Tonight?" It was strained, as though she was trying
to keep from shouting.

"Listen, Viv—"

"Why didn't you tell me? Why didn't you let me know?"

"I didn't know it myself. They never send me on the road this early."

And Darby remembered the way he had put his hand against the wall, as though he needed something to balance himself. Remembered all the details, the crisscross pattern of the dark green rug, the marble-topped table down there at the end of the hall. Four years ago, but he remembered everything.

Vivian said, "You can't go."

"I have no choice. It's my job."

"You listen to me. I say you can't go. You think for a minute I'll let you walk out—"

"Be reasonable. I give you my word—"

"Your word. I know how much that's worth." She said it with a trembling scorn. Then her voice broke. "Don't you have any conscience? How could you do this to me?"

The bridegroom retreated from the door. His face was pale and he was clenching and unclenching his hands. Trying to tell himself it wasn't anything. Knowing he was afraid to listen further. It was the most important day of his life and it mustn't be ruined. He returned to the guests, the party went on, and in the night, alone with his bride, he was able to dismiss the incident. It was such a minor thing, compared to the blinding delight of discovering how much she wanted him, how deeply she cared for him.

But now it was four years later and tonight he had been cured of the blindness. The pattern was clear, and the center of it was the face of Pete Lanson. It was significant that he hadn't seen Pete since the day of the wedding. Significant that she never mentioned Pete's name.

The pattern seemed to blaze. It became a screen that wouldn't burn even though it displayed the flame. He could see them on the screen, the two of them together while miles away downtown he slaved over columns of statistics to bring home the eighty-five per week. He could see them at opposite ends of a telephone wire, planning the next rendezvous, while he ate a hurried lunch so as to get back to the office and complete a report, hoping the report would meet with approval in the office upstairs, wishing plaintively it might result in a salary raise and he'd celebrate and buy her a bracelet or something. And in the pleasant weather of autumn and springtime, when he was trapped there at his desk, but content with the knowledge that she was waiting for him at home, she wasn't home at all. She was out visiting. Having herself a pleasant afternoon. With the shades pulled down and not a soul to bother them. Not even their own souls.

Then it was like a boiler bursting and Darby came up very slowly from the edge of the bed, his arms rising and his hands moving forward with the fingers spreading and curling, going toward the betrayer. He had full knowledge of what he was doing, told himself it wasn't possible, yet knew it was happening and he had no control over it. He saw the pair of white claws moving toward Vivian's throat, suddenly sensed the time was much later than that, it was all over and her sleep was permanent now. A white-hot flame went shooting into his eyes, and the horror staggered him.

But he hadn't touched her. Her shoulders rose and fell in the slow riding of slumber. Darby turned his face away and lifted himself into his bed. He felt the frosty sweat, the dismay at what he had almost done, knowing he was in a condition that made him capable of doing it.

He wondered if he was falling away from himself.

Chapter 3

Toward six in the morning he fell asleep, and an hour later he was under the shower. He never went for the Spartan routine of cold showers, but today he was in drastic need of a bracer, and the water splashed down on him like icy arrows. The brisk toweling put more life into him, then the shave, the tingle of witch hazel, and as he buttoned a clean white shirt and gazed up through the bedroom window at the morning sky, he felt more or less ready to face it.

In the breakfast nook he greeted Vivian pleasantly, sipped his orange juice, and turned to the sports page. There was another basketball scandal and a stable had burned in Kentucky, killing twelve thoroughbreds. Yale was swimming against Penn on Saturday, featuring a new sophomore free-style sensation, and Rocky Graziano had sprained his wrist in training.

From behind the barricade of the front page, Vivian told him that Washington wanted another increase in taxes, and he mumbled something to the effect that if it kept up like this, there'd soon be a tax on fresh air.

He ate a scrambled egg and a roll and two strips of crisp bacon. The coffee tasted especially strong this morning and he was glad of that. He always liked it strong and black. She poured him a second cup and then they sat there for a few minutes, smoking cigarettes and talking about Washington, and the mayor of Philadelphia, and a new housing development on Roosevelt Boulevard.

At the front door, as he buttoned the thick, fleecy raglan, she handed him his muffler. He thanked her, smiled at her, turned away sort of slowly, and heard the quiet click as the door closed behind him. Knowing she was watching him from the window.

During the bad weather, when the streets were icy, he never used the Plymouth. A bus took him to the Frankford elevated, which carried him downtown. In the elevated he scanned the advertising signs and wished they'd think up something new. That must be one hell of a soft job, writing the words for those cards. A middle-aged housewife showed him a jar of mayonnaise and screamed, "Delicious!" and that was the sum of the advertising copy. He shook his head slowly. Some people had it easy in this world. Ten or fifteen grand a year to think up words like "Delicious" and follow it with an exclamation point.

At the office, the large room where the actuaries sat at their desks and made arithmetical predictions concerning the death rate, the accident rate, the business losses that would come this year from fire and theft and other damage, he immersed himself in work. He was one of three assistants to a high-salaried actuary, a brilliant mathematician whose conversation consisted mostly of numbers and symbols and formulas. But that was just as well. It was the kind of job that placed emphasis on precision. They had to get with it and stay with it and they couldn't talk while they worked.

A tougher job than sitting at a typewriter and knocking off the word "Delicious!" He had worked on certain reports that had saved the insurance firm some hundreds of thousands of dollars. Last year, for instance, that paper dealing with fire hazard in the petroleum industry. As it turned out, they saved almost a million. Big numbers for a man making eighty-five per week.

Then it was twelve-thirty, and at the adjoining desk a stocky man grinned at him and told him to come on out and get some lunch. He grinned back at Harry Clawson and said O.K. It was always the best time of the day, the hour of having lunch with Harry.

Harry was his closest friend. They had gone to high school together, had played on the same sand-lot nine, then hadn't seen each other for several years while Harry was trying to enter big-league baseball and Darby drifted from one meaningless job to another. Until they found themselves in the same classroom, in the evening school where they were taught insurance, and statistics, and what necktie to wear when applying for employment.

That was important, that necktie angle. It was part of what the instructor called "the Chestnut Street look." As the instructor put it, Chestnut Street in Philadelphia is on a parallel with Madison Avenue in New York, or Beacon Street in Boston, or Pennsylvania Avenue in Washington. And so he and Harry had gone out and purchased the right kind of necktie, the right cut of worsted, the shoes that didn't have too much gloss.

He and Harry had acquired "the Chestnut Street look" and had never lost it. As they merged with the lunchtime throng, the solemn Philadelphia faces coming out of insurance offices, advertising agencies, investment houses, they walked along Chestnut Street with a certain relaxed dignity. There was nothing flaunted about it, they had no idea it was there, and yet it added up to a suggestion of aloofness, just a touch of snobbery that wasn't really undemocratic, merely set them off from the loud glitter of Market Street, the saloons along Arch, and of course the flophouses in that other world, that tenderloin world of Eighth and Race.

Harry pulled at an unlit brier and said, "We'll have more snow tonight. Look at it up there."

Darby glanced up. The sky was heavy and getting dark. It looked like an endless field of dark ice.

A traffic cop blew his whistle and they stood at the curb at Seventh and Chestnut and saw the cars breaking loose on Seventh Street. A taxi started a right-hand turn and had to stop for pedestrians crossing Chestnut Street, Horns began to honk.

"No system," Harry said. "Look at that jam."

Darby tightened his muffler against the biting wind. "How are Gert and the kids?"

"They're fine." Harry had four children and his wife was expecting a fifth. "When you and Viv coming over?"

He smiled. "We're socially lazy."

"Lazy, period," Harry chided. "Too much trouble to get the car out."

"We'll be over soon." He wished the traffic light would

turn green. He was in a hurry to cross the street, in a
hurry to have his lunch and get back to the desk. As
though having lunch with Harry had suddenly changed
from a pleasure to an ordeal.

The light turned green and they crossed the street and
went into a restaurant that featured a rustic, sort-of-
British décor. The tables were oak and most of the
patrons were men. They found a booth and a waitress
handed them the menus.

Harry ordered a bowl of snapper soup, roast beef rare
with mashed potatoes and string beans, and a salad. He
asked the waitress if they had pumpkin pie, and she said
yes, and he told her to save him a cut.

After that it was quiet. It seemed that everything was
quiet in the restaurant and on the street outside.

Until he heard Harry saying, "Come on, wake up."

In front of his eyes the menu was a spinning card that
made a beige blur and floated toward him, went away,
floated in again.

Harry indicated the badge on the waitress' starched
blouse. The badge had her name on it, and Harry said,
"Miss Dennis is waiting."

He raised his eyes and saw Miss Dennis waiting there.
She was trying to be patient and she smiled tolerantly.
But her pencil tapped the pad.

"Coffee," he said.

Harry leaned forward. "What? What's that?"

The menu fell away from his hands and dropped off the
edge of the table. Miss Dennis bent over and picked it up.

"I'm sorry," he said. He closed his eyes and wanted to
keep them closed. "Just bring me a cup of black coffee."

Harry frowned. "Is that all?"

He nodded. A slow, weary nod, as though he scarcely
had the strength to move his head.

The waitress had walked away from the table. He saw
Harry staring at him.

"What's wrong?" Harry asked. "You sick?"

"No."

"Then what is it? What's wrong?"

He had to say something. He focused on a salt shaker

in the center of the table. "I don't know." But that
sounded a little silly, even to himself. "I just don't have
any appetite."

"You seemed all right when we left the office."

He put his elbows on the table. "Maybe I'm smoking
too much."

"How much?"

He saw Harry looking at him in a way that was irritat-
ing. As if Harry was probing. As if it was any of Harry's
concern. Then all at once he realized the importance of
hiding this thing from Harry. Hiding it from everyone.
He mustn't allow his demeanor to give him away. Sooner
or later it would come out in the open, but for the present
he had a good reason for keeping it quiet.

"Three packs a day," he said evenly. Then frowned and
shook his head, a self-reprimand for too much tobacco. "I
just can't stop."

"Sure you can. Use a little will power."

It was relatively easy to bluff it through this way, because he actually consumed between two and three packs
a day and there were times when he had worried about
it and tried to cut down. He grinned at Harry and said,
"No use kidding myself. They got me licked."

The waitress arrived with the black coffee and Harry's
snapper soup. Darby lifted the menu, scanned it, and
heard Harry saying, "That's the idea, that's the boy."

"Ham and cabbage," Darby told the waitress.

Miss Dennis smiled dimly and wrote it down. She
walked away with her starched skirt rustling primly.

Harry thumbed in her direction and murmured, "You
know something? That isn't bad."

"Nice legs," Darby said automatically, just to stay on
the beam with Harry. Then he wondered whether Miss
Dennis really had nice legs.

Harry provided the reassuring answer. "It shows in the
ankles. You look at the ankles and you can tell if they're
streamlined all the way up."

Usually, when Harry talked in that vein, it was somewhat annoying to Darby and he always steered the topic
onto another track. Not that he was prudish; he could

appreciate a dirty joke if it was clever enough, and he could accept four-letter words if they were timed right. But he never liked it when it was cheap and artificial. It was all right to admire an attractive woman, but not as though she were in the open market for a five-dollar session.

Yet now he didn't mind Harry's talk. Somehow it was stimulating and there was a flavor in it that tempted him and caused him to ask, "How does it show in the ankles?"

"That's where the curve starts," Harry replied. "That's where you look first. To get an estimate. Then you decide just what they have and what they'll do with it."

And Harry was sitting there with his Chestnut Street look, with the clean white shirt and the dark blue tie with tiny polka dots. With the conservative cut of gray flannel, the bowl of the brier pipe only moderately displayed above the breast pocket. Harry Clawson, the respectable family man, the father of four children.

If it had been yesterday, he would have told himself that Harry was a hypocrite and a lecher, even though Harry never went further than just talking about it.

Yet now it was today, and history had changed greatly since last night. And Darby sat there with his own Chestnut Street look, wearing the clean white shirt and a solid-color bottle-green tie, with a salt-and-pepper Scotch tweed, tailored, as Dominic advertised, "for the man who places emphasis on good taste." He sat there and smiled thinly and said, "I imagine Miss Dennis doesn't do it often. But when she does it, it's something."

"There's a way to find out, you know." Harry's grin was wicked.

Darby nodded seriously. "I think I will."

Harry chuckled. It was strictly stag-party stuff and of course it was just talk.

But then Darby said, "I really mean to find out."

Harry stopped chuckling. One corner of his mouth came up, one side of his face frowned at Darby while the other side tried to hold a grin. "You sound like you want to do business."

His tone was even. "Any reason why not?"

Harry made it a complete frown. "Hey, boy, for God's sake."

"Here she comes now." Darby gazed coolly down the row of tables. "You just sit there and listen."

Miss Dennis came down the aisle and expertly placed the rare roast beef in front of Harry. She lowered the plate of ham and cabbage to the table and saw the man with straw-colored hair sending his hazel eyes into her face. The hazel eyes had a certain purity and wanted nothing more than to pity her, and asked her to pity him.

"Forgive me," Darby said.

Miss Dennis blinked awkwardly. "For what?"

"We were talking about you."

Harry sat up straighter. "Hey, listen—"

But he paid no attention to Harry. And Miss Dennis didn't know Harry was there. She was receiving the gentle caress of the man's hazel eyes and seeing the clean line of his lips. She wondered at the sudden tenderness that flowed within her, wondered at the sudden realization that her life was dull and lonely, but that it didn't have to be that way.

And found herself saying, "I know what you mean. They always size up the poor waitresses."

"That's so, isn't it? Why do we do that?"

She completely forgot there were other tables to wait on. Her smile was thoughtful. "Sometimes the waitresses size up the customers."

They didn't hear Harry's weak, embarrassed laugh that broke off and became a cough.

Darby's lips moved slightly, as though he were touching her smile with his lips. "Maybe it's just a game we play when we're unhappy. You think maybe that's it?"

"I'll think about it," she said with utmost truthfulness. "I'll let you know later."

Then she moved away from the table, moved backward a little, still looking at him. Until another table called to her and she walked off like someone walking alone through a dark wood, seeking someone.

"Well," Harry said. "I'll be goddamed."

"You see how easy it is?" But he didn't mean that. The

words were only a sound, the voice of just another lewd
bastard making conversation with Harry. The thoughts
beyond the voice were pure thoughts of Miss Dennis, kind
thoughts and sort of sad, pitying her and wishing he were
in a position to give her some happiness.

And Harry was saying, with a sort of odd admiration,
"What's come over you? All of a sudden you're a first-
class operator."

The thoughts remained with Miss Dennis. The voice
only played with Harry. "I took a correspondence course."

"You did? Then this lad enrolls tomorrow. I'll tell you
something. That was smooth. Perfect timing. Couldn't
be smoother."

The final word was a sudden turn in the road. Smoother. It was an acute turn that took him away from Miss
Dennis and dropped him down and far away from everything as he remembered the smooth looks and smooth
voice of Pete Lanson.

And he said, "Oh, yes, it could. We've both known
smoother operators."

Harry sliced himself a chunk of blood-red meat. He put
it into his mouth, chewed it diligently, swallowed it, and
began to butter a roll. "Like who, for instance?"

It had to be handled delicately. Get to it gradually.
Let it ride along easily so that presently Harry would take
the wheel. Harry had been very close to Pete Lanson.

Darby said, "Well, let's see. Remember Charley Webster?"

"That loudmouth? He had as much finesse as a push-
cart huckster."

"What about Frank Gannon?"

Harry shook his head emphatically. "Just a cave man.
He thought he was scaring them." Then, as though he
were conducting a quiz program, "Come on, try again."

Darby sent a half-smile toward the restaurant ceiling.
"Let's see now," and let it drift into a pause.

It became a long pause and finally Harry broke it. "I'll
tell you who. I'd say the slickest of them all was Pete
Lanson."

Darby allowed the smile to widen. His slow nod was

full agreement. Then it occurred to him he ought to temper it just a little, and he inclined his head dubiously and murmured, "Well, now, wait a minute—"

"Wait my eye. That Pete was the boy, I tell you. Every move he made was pure velvet. From the very first hello he'd have them dizzy."

And only mildly curious, "What was it? What did he have?"

Harry shrugged. "The natural gift. Like Musial swings at bat. Like Ray Robinson fights. Comes natural, that's all. There's no effort, and that's what they go for."

"And Pete had that?"

"In solid black spades." Then a grin, slightly twisted. "He had it in spades and never gave diamonds. And always busted the hearts."

"Ouch!" Meaning the pun. "But do you think the hearts stayed busted? Think they remember these smooth operators?"

"They don't forget easily." Harry thought about it a moment.

"You think they still dream about him?"

"Probably. Either that or they see him whenever they go to the movies. And look at the lad on the screen. The silky glamour boy."

"Only the dumb ones do that," Darby said. "The smarter ones want the real thing again."

Harry's chuckle was on the sharp side. It had meaning. "I know one thing for sure. Pete would be available."

"He didn't get married?"

"He'll never get married. Unless—"

"Unless what?" he interrupted very quickly, throwing it like a dart.

Then he was sitting there rigidly, waiting for Harry's reply. Seeing the strange look in Harry's eyes. And wondering if Harry knew. After all, in situations such as this, almost everyone knew except the husband. He thought of the ancient saying, "The husband is always the last to find out."

But suddenly it made no difference whether Harry knew or not. He wasn't even looking at Harry.

He was looking across the row of tables and seeing Miss Dennis standing near the window facing Chestnut Street. Beyond the window, far up there in the sullen gray sky, the sun had managed to break through, and it sent a dazzling ray through the plate glass, doing something to the wavy light brown hair of Miss Dennis. Changing the color of her hair, making it platinum blonde.

Darby shuddered. A heavy weight was pressed against his eyes. He was remembering the uncanny moment of last night when it seemed that Vivian's hair had changed color from dark brown to silver yellow. And silver yellow was just another way of saying platinum blonde.

He told himself he'd better throw away this platinum-blonde routine. It certainly had nothing to do with the issue at hand, the burning issue of his wife and another man.

Just then he heard someone laughing softly, and looked up and saw that it was Harry.

"I was just thinking," Harry chuckled. "When Pete was in high school he did it with the principal's wife."

Darby smiled, but only with his lips. His eyes were expressionless. His eyes stared past Henry and saw nothing. While other eyes, planted deep in his brain, saw the pleasant scene of Pete Lanson getting murdered.

Chapter 4

It was snowing when he left the office at five-fifteen. On the ride home in the elevated, he watched the increasing swiftness of the snowfall. He told himself it would soon be a blizzard.

At five-fifty, as he put his key in the lock and opened the front door, he enjoyed the idea of entering a warm house, getting away from the knifing wind and snow, the raging storm.

But then it was strange. In the very process of taking off his coat, he wanted to keep it on and go out again. He didn't want to think about the reason, or whether there was a reason; he just felt like going out and taking a walk in the snowstorm.

Vivian came into the living room and said hello and told him that dinner would be ready in a few minutes. He nodded, and that was all. He scarcely looked at her. But he listened attentively to the sound of her receding footsteps as she went back to the kitchen. As though each sound she made were significant.

Because now it was sharply necessary that he pay close attention to every move she made. Listen with a keen ear. And watch her like a hawk.

The bitch. The miserable, low-down, cheating tramp. And he felt the impulse to force a showdown here and now. Just as if all the proof were out in the open, on the table. As if he had seen, with his own eyes, the filthy trick that was being played on him.

He sat on the sofa and picked up the evening paper and tried to concentrate on the headlines. He couldn't do it. He found himself concentrating on last night, and the way she'd given him the look that said, I want you, I want you. And all the while laughing at him and saying to herself, Oh, well, I'll try to be real sweet about it and let him go on thinking he's the only one.

He wondered what kept him from lunging into the kitchen and breaking every bone in her body.

Just then he heard her calling to him. Dinner was ready.

He stood up, trembling. He told himself to relax and play it cool. He stood there working very hard, trying to relax, and managed to light a cigarette. Then he walked out of the living room and down the hall. Just like any other husband going in to have dinner with his wife.

Dinner was thirty minutes of just eating the food and listening to the radio playing recorded music. But every now and then he glanced up from his plate, expecting to catch her at something. Maybe watching him to see if he was suspicious, or maybe a distant look in her eyes that would say she wished her dinner companion were someone else.

Yet all he saw was the energetic action of her knife and fork as she sat there enjoying her meal.

Then, when dinner was over, he offered to help with the dishes. Just to stay there in the kitchen and keep an eye on her.

And he listened carefully to her calm refusal of the offer as she said, "No, thanks. It's very nice of you. But after all, you're tired. You worked hard today."

He frowned. "How do you know?"

With the same calmness, "You told me they're rushing you at the office. Said you were knocking yourself out."

His frown deepened. "When did I say that?"

"Last night." Just the trace of a smile. "Don't you remember?"

He blinked hard, and got rid of the frown. But his eyes were hard and icy. "Yes, I remember. What about it?"

She shrugged. "Nothing." She shrugged again. "Nothing at all."

He turned and started to leave the kitchen.

Then it was like a hook reaching out and hauling him back as he heard her saying, "Except that I didn't believe you."

He whirled on her and opened his mouth and then realized he didn't know what to say. He pivoted abruptly and walked out of the kitchen.

In the living room he turned the dial that brightened a television screen and tried to focus on it, tried to laugh at the antics of two men wearing checkered suits and straw hats. They were doing their best to be funny, but he watched them as though they were a couple of mosquitoes buzzing around and getting on his nerves.

Then the program changed, and it was a quiz show, one of the few that he usually liked, but now he wasn't even looking at it. He was staring at the floor. He heard Vivian come in and sit down at the other end of the sofa and he went on staring at the floor.

The program changed again. A musical variety, with singers and dancers who had rehearsed every day for a week, just for this hour, but he was looking at the screen as though there were nothing on it.

He heard the station announcement that said it was ten-thirty. He pulled himself up from the sofa, went into the hall, and took his coat from the closet. He jabbed his arms through the sleeves of the coat and quickly buttoned it and started toward the front door.

His path was crossed by a flashing of dark hair and white face and blue dress as Vivian blocked his progress to the door.

She put her hands on her hips and said, "Just where do you think you're going?"

"Out." And the tone was as curt and final as the word.

"Where?" She snapped it at him.

For a moment he couldn't talk. Then, his head thrust forward, he shouted at her, "I'm going out for a walk. Do you mind?"

She held back a reply, just looked him up and down. Then she prodded with her thumb, over her shoulder, to indicate the blizzard out there, and said, "You mean to tell me you're going for a walk? Going out in that weather?"

He stared past her, at the door window, and saw the white fury of the snowstorm. As it raged, it seemed to beckon, and he said, "I like to walk around in the snow. Anything wrong in that?"

She didn't answer. Her eyes were a set of drills that tried to penetrate his head and find out what was going on inside.

And he said to her, without sound, You'll find out, you bitch. You'll find out soon enough.

His voice made the cold stab: "I just want to get out of the house for a while."

"Why?"

"Why?" He mimicked her tone with a sneering grimace. "What is it, a big deal? What do I have to do, write out an explanation?"

She took a deep breath and closed her eyes for a moment. Then, her lips set tightly, her voice grimly quiet, "Take off your coat."

"What?" He was shouting again. "What's that?"

"You heard me. I said take off your coat. You're not walking out of this house."

He winced with the sudden and staggering knowledge that something was definitely out of kilter. It seemed the situation was being turned inside out.

But the feeling lasted only for an instant. He hurled it away as he moved toward the door.

Vivian wouldn't step aside.

"Get out of my way," he said, "or I'll knock you down."

She didn't budge.

"All right," he muttered, "you're asking for it."

And went on going toward the door and told himself it would be a collision. And he didn't care. He realized that he sort of liked the idea of bumping into her and knocking her down. Yet just as he reached her, her arms moved quickly and she gave him a violent shove that sent him reeling backward.

He almost fell. The wall stopped him. He leaned back against it, somewhat stupefied, as he stared at Vivian and saw her eyes flashing, her breasts heaving.

"Now you'll stop playing games," she blazed. "You'll damn well tell me what this is all about."

Without moving from where he stood, he was trying

to fight his way through a thick fog, while a blunt voice deep inside told him that he didn't really know what it was all about.

"Tell me," she demanded. "I have a right to know what's going on."

He stumbled through the strange fog and all at once it was gone and he was telling himself that everything was clear again, in sharp focus. She was clever, all right, and her display of rage had almost succeeded in curtaining her fear. But now, as he smiled thinly and studied her eyes, he could see the fear, the desperation.

He turned away from her and walked into the living room, but he didn't take off his coat. Just made a smooth manipulation with a book of matches and a cigarette, and held onto the thin smile as he let the smoke drift from his lips.

Vivian followed him across the carpet. He stood with his back to her, and took a debonair drag at the cigarette, and murmured, "It's really too bad you had to lose your temper."

"I didn't lose my temper," she said. Then, feverishly, "Can't you see what's happening? I'm just trying to reach you, that's all."

"Reach me?" He turned to face her, and his smile was thinner now. "What do you mean by that?"

"You're a million miles away."

"Am I?" His eyebrows were raised. "Well, maybe I am. I wonder who sent me there."

"That's what I'm wondering."

His lips were tight. The smile was gone. "You don't have to look far to find out."

She stepped back and winced, as though he'd actually jabbed her with a needle. "You mean it's me? I've done something?" Then bluntly, challengingly, "All right, let's have it out. Tell me what I've done."

"We won't go into that," he said. "It's just a waste of time. You'll only deny it."

She took another backward step. Her eyes were wide, staring uncomprehendingly at the floor. And then she frowned. And finally she glared at him and shouted,

"You know I haven't done anything. What kind of stunt are you trying to pull?"

He didn't reply.

"Answer me," she shouted.

He moved toward the window, looked out, and murmured, "Let's talk about the climate. I think Philadelphia has a lousy climate. If I were rich I'd buy a house in Florida."

"You answer me," she blazed.

He went on looking out the window and murmured mildly, "It's a pity what winter does to the street cleaners. Tomorrow they'll be shoveling snow all day long."

Then he sort of drifted away from what was going on in the room and he pictured the platoons of old men who wearily shoveled snow while more snow kept coming down, making their task endless. But maybe it wasn't as bad as all that. Maybe they actually liked the work, and were luckier than all the rich people who ran away from the snow and went to Florida and got bored with sitting in the sun and doing nothing.

He heard the angry voice that dragged him back to the room saying, "I'm wise to your game. I know what you're trying to do."

He turned slowly and looked at her, his eyebrows raised inquiringly, his lips once again smiling thinly.

"You think you're clever," Vivian raged. "But you're not putting anything over. I know I haven't done anything wrong. But I'm not so sure about you."

His lips went down at the corners. His brows lowered. "Me?"

"Yes, you." She took slow steps, coming toward him.

His arms were stiff at his sides. His fists were clenched.

She came up close to him and said, "You've done something to make you feel guilty. And you're trying to take it out on me."

It was nothing more than a string of words, spoken in a lower, much calmer tone than her previous angry exclamations. And yet, as he heard it, the weight and force of it was like a huge rock crashing down on his head. He grimaced and shut his eyes tightly.

He stared at the black screen of his lowered eyelids, and saw, unable to believe that he was seeing it, a face that came onto the screen.

He had no idea whose face it was. The features were much too vague. But the hair was long and wavy and he knew it was a girl. A platinum blonde.

He groaned. "Oh, no. No."

He opened his eyes to see Vivian's whitened face, felt her hands gripping his shoulders, and heard her saying, "What is it? For God's sake, what's the matter with you?"

He took hold of her wrists and hurled her aside with a violence that threw her to the floor. He didn't hear the fall, or Vivian's cry of shock and pain and fright.

He just told himself he had to get out of there, and hurried to the front door.

There was nothing at all in his eyes as he walked out of the house.

Chapter 5

His head was lowered and his shoulders were hunched as he advanced slowly against the onrush of the blizzard. He looked down at his feet and grinned slyly at the thick-soled Norwegian moccasins that were guaranteed waterproof, then tightened the muffler around his throat and buttoned the flaps of his gloves. He told himself he was perfectly equipped for this pleasant stroll through the snow. He'd just walk around for a while until he got tired and then go home and get a good night's sleep.

He lifted his head to peer through the swirling snow and get his bearings, trying to estimate how many minutes it had been since he had left the house. But this street didn't look familiar, and for some reason it was impossible to measure time. The dial of his wrist watch was frosted and he couldn't see the numbers. He moved his finger toward the glass, to rub off the frost, but just then his attention was drawn to something more important, a bright light down at the end of the block.

He headed toward the lit window. It was nothing more than a candy store. Why was it important for him to go into a candy store? He certainly didn't feel like eating candy, and he had cigarettes in his pocket. Maybe he was just going in there to get warm. But no. He was a long way from freezing. It was really quite comfortable out here in the blizzard.

He entered the store. It was very small. It was empty. He stood at the counter and stared at the neat array of penny and nickel candy. Then a tiny old man came in from a back room and asked him what he wanted.

"I don't know," he said, and smiled sort of sadly because it was all too true.

45

The old man shrugged, and made a plaintive little gesture that indicated the limited variety of merchandise. He murmured, "Just look around. There's no hurry."

Darby's face stiffened. "Don't get sarcastic."

"Me?" The old man seemed to get smaller. "I'm not sarcastic, mister. I only said—"

"I heard what you said."

The old man looked him up and down. The weary old eyes saw this younger citizen standing there wearing a raglan coat and looking fairly respectable. But after all, it was hard to tell. And then again, it was late at night and he'd never seen this person before.

Darby's tone was flat and metallic. "What are you looking at?"

That more or less did it. The old man started to back away.

"No," Darby said, "don't do that."

"Please, mister—"

"Please what?" He frowned puzzledly. "What are you afraid of?"

"Mister," and the old man swallowed hard, "it's just a little store. I don't make much money here. Just enough to get along. Me and my wife—"

"Your wife?" Darby cut in. "You have a wife?"

"Sure," the old man said, and his worry moved onto another track as he told himself it was a crazy world these days and anything could happen.

Darby heard his own voice saying slowly and carefully, "Does your wife ever cheat on you?"

The old man took a deep breath. "Mister. Please. My wife is sixty-eight years old."

"All right," Darby said. "But still, she's a woman. And these women, they're clever. Believe me when I tell you they're clever as snakes. They know all the tricks." And then he looked up at the ceiling and threw a laugh at it, a harsh and sour laugh. "They'll cut your heart out at the drop of a hat. Then, when it comes to a showdown, what happens? Does she admit the truth?"

"Mister. Mister—"

"Don't interrupt. This is important. Listen carefully.

I know what I'm talking about. I tell you it just can't be done, you can't get her to admit the truth. She stands there like Joan of Arc. Tells me I have a guilty conscience and I'm trying to take it out on her."

The old man took a tentative step forward. "Look, mister, if you need another drink, there's a taproom—"

"Who's looking for a taproom? And besides, I don't drink. And I don't gamble. I don't run around. So where does she get that guilty business? What have I got to feel guilty about?"

The old man felt safer now, and somewhat bolder. He took another step forward and pointed to a clock on the wall. "It's getting late. It's time for me to close up."

But Darby didn't hear that. His eyes were closed and again there was the black screen. And the face on the screen. The girl. The platinum blonde.

He told himself to open his eyes. But it seemed that something was wrong with his eyelids and he couldn't raise them. Well, all right then, try another trick, just stop thinking about it, get away from it. Get away, for God's sake, and come back to the issue at hand. Don't look at anything but the issue, the ice-cold, white-hot issue of being married to a woman who performed matinees with another man.

The trick worked. The platinum blonde went away. He was able to open his eyes. In the instant that he did so, he bluntly told himself to get the issue decided. Go ahead and settle it.

He told himself there was only one way to settle it.

He wished there were another way, but there wasn't. Just this one method, a simple and easy transaction that would put a stop to the matinees.

"Mister, please. I want to close up the store."

But he didn't hear that, either. His eyes aimed at two large books, one gray and one yellow, resting on a shelf under the pay phone. He picked up the gray book and leafed the pages until he found the page he wanted, then ran his finger down the list of names and finally hit it: "Lanson Peter drugs."

The address told him his man owned a store downtown

in the tenderloin section, the dismal real estate down there around Eighth and Race.

He moved toward the door. The old man eagerly opened it for him, and he walked out and noticed that the snow had stopped falling and the wind had slackened. He started down the block, walking very fast.

He walked and walked, until finally he saw a taxi and hailed it and climbed in and said, "Take me home."

"That's easy," the driver said. "Just tell me where you live."

He leaned forward and slipped off the seat and fell to his knees. "Damn it," he said, and got back on the seat and muttered, "Where the hell are we?"

"Philadelphia."

"Don't be a wise guy."

"On a night like this," the driver complained, "I have to pick up a drunk."

"I'm not drunk. What street are we on? What hundred?"

"Second Street. Twenty-six hundred block."

"You're crazy."

"All right," the driver said. "I'm crazy."

But then Darby looked again at the street and the houses, and knew it was far down on Second Street, near the big intersection at Front and Lehigh. He had walked seven or eight miles.

He said, "Take me to the corner of Eighth and Race."

The driver frowned. "Is that where you live?"

For a long moment he just gazed blankly at the driver. Then he grinned. "Yes," he said. "That's exactly where I live."

The driver shrugged and turned to the wheel and the taxi moved. It made a turn and went onto Front Street, went down Front, turned again and went down Sixth all the way to Vine, then across Vine to Eighth, and down Eighth to Race. As Darby paid the fare, he glanced at his wrist watch and saw it was past three in the morning. He saw the taxi riding away and stood there in the snow and told himself he was down here on the corner of Eighth and Race.

He was here in the core of the tenderloin. And at first he couldn't see them, the street seemed empty. But then he made out the shapes, the dim shapes huddled against dark walls. He saw the slumped shoulders and the lowered heads, and some of them sitting in doorways with their elbows on their knees. He saw them in the dirty glow of yellow lamps in unwashed windows.

Like dead men, strangely able to breathe and move even though they had died long ago. He looked at them and wondered vaguely what they were doing out here in the freezing weather. He didn't realize that his coat was unbuttoned and that he wasn't wearing his gloves— the gloves he had taken off in the taxi and left on the seat. So he walked north on Eighth Street, not feeling the cold, feeling only the closeness of the walls on both sides of Skid Row.

There was a certain comfort in the closeness of the walls. They were the walls of restaurants, the windows daring a man to come in and eat, if he could stand the food. And the walls of flophouses where it cost a quarter a night and no extra charge for the bugs. The walls of missions that provided a bowl of soup and salvation, and the walls covered with bright-colored posters that invited them to come in and see, for only twenty cents, a movie made twelve years ago. There were all these walls, and certain other walls of certain unsigned houses that contained, the broken bricks said, three floors of rooms where there were no limits, no rules, and anything could go on.

"Mister—"

He turned and saw the creased throat, the purple face, the wild mane of gray hair. And the eyes that had no special hue and couldn't seem to focus.

"Mister, I don't want coffee."

And in a nearby doorway, someone laughed.

The purple face paid no attention. "I don't want coffee, I don't want a meal. I don't even want subway fare."

The laugh again, with a cough in it.

"I'll tell you what I want. I want a drink of wine."

Looking down at the Norwegian moccasins that cost every bit of $19.75. Then up along the fine thick tweed, woven in Scotland and tailored by Dominic for $115. Looking at the man who wore a fine raglan and belonged on Chestnut Street.

Darby gave him fifty cents. He watched him going away and heard the shape rising in the doorway, the voice not laughing any more, the voice saying seriously, "Could you count me in?"

It was a skinny young man with a mean face, one eye made of glass improperly fitted. The other eye was narrow and wary, like the eye of a fox.

"Come on, I saw you gave him half a buck. You got more."

He started to close in, the living eye scarcely moving, yet taking in both side of the street, both ends of the block.

"Keep away," Darby said, and readied himself.

The young man was uncertain. His hand was near his pocket where the blade rested, but another pocket held parole papers, and he wondered if it was worth the risk.

"No offense, mister."

"All right," Darby said. "Here's a quarter," and handed it to him.

"Thanks."

Darby started away, came back, and said, "Where's Lanson's drugstore?" wondering what had caused him to forget the address in the phone book.

"Lanson?" The living eye looked up. "Oh, yeah. Pete." The skinny arm pointed north. "Up a block and a half and turn right. Just off the corner."

A cat came out of an alley, took a look at all the snow, and went back in. Farther on up the street a fat man, aproned and puffing, emerged from a restaurant and whiffed the cold air and gazed yearningly at the sky. As though even the dreams were up there, much too far away. Darby passed the fat man, crossed Vine, and saw three colored men wearing caps, their hands in overcoat pockets. They stood in a row, leaning against a wall, and it seemed they were sleeping standing up, until he saw their opened eyes and moving lips.

He heard only a part of it.

"—tell me that chick was high. Don't tell me that."

"Man, I was there. I know."

"But you were high. So how could you know?"

Then music came from a radio beyond a shuttered window, and more music from a juke box in a café that had only one customer. He saw the customer putting in another nickel and sensed the box would play the same tune. Maybe it had been playing it for hours, because it was that kind of tune. Something about leaves that would never live again because spring would never come again, for you are gone, you are gone, and I'm alone.

He walked away from the sad song and turned the corner and saw the sign above the window, the sign reading, "Pete's Cut-Rate Drugs."

The window was dark except for the thin green fire of a neon border. It displayed pyramids of patent medicines, cards that said prices were slashed, and look at this, only sixty-nine cents, two boxes for the price of one. The window seemed much too small for all the merchandise it showed, but there it was, the complete array. And every buy a terrific value.

Then he peered through the glass door and saw that the store was roomy, the counters neatly stacked, the floor swept clean, and everything in order. All set for tomorrow's customers. The store seemed to boast quietly that it did a profitable business. He stood there thinking of the money coming into the store, the smooth merchandising of the man behind the counter, the easy smile and the satiny voice suggesting an extra bottle of this, and try this new brand of razor blades, and buy the large-size tube, it adds up cheaper in the long run.

He stood there wishing it wasn't this hour of three-thirty in the morning. Wishing it was nine or ten, or whatever hour was closing time, so the man would be in there alone. Knowing it would happen quickly, before the man would know it was happening. Do it quickly and neatly, just another smooth transaction in the clean store where everything was neat and smooth. With the floor thoroughly scrubbed and everything in order.

Well, here it was. And it would be here tomorrow. But as he thought of tomorrow, and what he planned to do, he felt the pressure of knowing it had reached the point where he had no choice. He had to do it. And his head became heavy with the anxiety of wondering just how to go about it. If he handled it right, there'd be no need to face a jury; the thing would be unsolved and they'd attribute the deed to one of the meaner citizens of the tenderloin. He asked himself if he really had that kind of talent, the talent to handle it with sufficient finesse and precision and split-second timing.

At first the answer was no; he was untried at this sort of thing. Not even a novice. But somewhere in the middle of his negative answer, a wire threw off sparks that said yes, and the sparks grew and became dominant. He realized that the cunning would come automatically. Like the cunning of an animal that couldn't survive unless it did away with a particular quarry. And so it was yes, a definite yes. And that added more pressure.

Because it took away the final excuse for not diving off the high board. So that now, just as sure as his feet stood in snow that was real, the issue was real and he was going to do it.

The finality of it began to frighten him. He turned away from the store front, as though just standing there and looking inside had been part of the deed itself. As though the street was too empty, too dark, and the quiet was stifling. He walked anxiously toward the corner, wanting to see someone, anyone, wanting to get away from the lonely depths where the only companion was a weird party who wore a raglan coat and had straw-colored hair.

He turned the corner and saw the three colored men. He saw more men on the other side of the street, and still more farther on down, and here and there a woman, mean drunk or happy drunk or maybe just a little drunk, just enough to be plain fed up with everything. He

walked on down the street, trying to make contact with
the faces. But they didn't see him. Until one of them, a
woman with red-rimmed eyes and a broken nose, looked
him up and down with dull resentment, the eyes saying,
Out slumming? Go on, go back where you belong.

He needed contact, needed it badly, but he couldn't
find it here on the faces along Skid Row. There was
nothing he could say to them; their eyes were too frozen
or too hazy with alcohol. Even if they wanted a handout,
that was all they wanted from him. Beyond that, they
regarded him as just another well-dressed trifler, fooling
around in a world they took seriously. Because they had
to take it seriously. There was no other world for them
to live in.

On Race Street he saw the orange and lavender lights
of an after-hour club. But there was no one at the door,
no one to ask him for a membership card. If he carried
money, he was welcome. He went in. The place was
on a slightly higher level than the average tenderloin
saloon. But still he saw no faces that offered contact.
For the most part, the men and women were paired up,
and those who weren't paired up were having a private
meeting with themselves and looked as though they
didn't want to be bothered.

Just to do something, he put a quarter in a machine
and received a pack of cigarettes. He stood there reading
the printed warning under the cellophane, "—nor to re-
move the contents of this package without destroying
said stamp, under the penalties provided by law in such
cases."

He read it again. He studied it as though it were
something important that had to be studied. He saw the
words under the cellophane, the words "destroying" and
"penalties," and suddenly he visualized, in one mixed
scene, the act of destruction and the enactment of the
penalty.

He had to talk to someone. He had to hear a voice that
would lift the black curtain and let him look at the
normal view. His legs felt unsteady and he moved in a
sort of weaving path toward the bar, wondering what he

would do when he got there. Then he saw, along the opposite wall, the three phone booths.

In that instant he knew what he had to do. A dazzling light was showing him the way. It was so simple, so logical. And he would hear the voice, the one voice he needed to hear. Her sleepy hello at three-forty-five in the morning. The voice of Vivian.

Telling him to come home, and they'd talk it over, and everything would be all right. And being able to prove to him that he was on a wrong track, there was no third person at all, just herself and her husband. Proving to him it had been that way from the beginning, was that way now, and would always be that way. Helping him to find the reason for absurd suspicions and wild thoughts, the insane thoughts that had almost led to an insane act.

The nearest phone booth was a place of safety, of warm sweet refuge. He went in and closed the door, sobbed the immense silent sob of utter relief as he told himself it was all right now, it was really all right. He dropped the nickel in and dialed the number.

He got a busy signal. But it couldn't be. Not at this hour.

He told himself he must have dialed the wrong number. He put the nickel in and tried again. And heard the busy signal again.

He tried it again. And again and again and again. He sat there listening to the busy signal that drilled through his brain and caused him to grit his teeth, as if the drill were white-hot metal.

He went on trying the number until his finger ached from turning the dial. The face of his wrist watch told him it was ten minutes past four. Very early in the morning. Very late in the day.

He opened the door of the phone booth and started to slide himself out, he saw the camel's-hair coat emerging from the adjoining booth, saw the black hair, slick but not greasy, and watched the easy stride as the man passed the bar and moved toward the front door. And then the man half turned, waving good night to someone, and there it was, the profile, the smooth line of brow and nose and lips.

The lips that only a few moments ago had spoken into a phone, saying good night to Vivian.

The smiling lips of Pete Lanson.

Chapter 6

IT WAS VERY COLD in the phone booth, much colder
than the January weather in the streets. He put a cigarette in his mouth, struck a match, and watched the
match flaming. The flame crawled down to his pressed
fingers and for a moment he didn't feel it. Then the
burning came and he dropped the match. He struck another, lit the cigarette, left the phone booth, and started
toward the door. As he neared the door, he saw the platinum blonde.

She sat alone, in that dimly lit corner where all the
other tables were empty. In front of her an empty glass
waited to be filled again, and she was sitting there pa-
tiently, just like the glass, waiting for someone to come
along and fill it.

There wasn't much paint, just lipstick and a little
powder. The platinum-blonde hair was fluffy and then
lost the fluffiness where the brilliantine smoothed it back
along the temples, behind the ears. She wore dangling
earrings that turned up at the ends, sort of following
the quiet arrogance of her turned-up nose and the upward sweep of her bulging breasts.

Her gray-green eyes told Darby to go ahead and look
her over, to take all the time he wanted. It wouldn't be
an ordinary purchase, her eyes said, even after four in
the morning when business was apt to be slack. So here
it is. Take it or leave it.

He approached the table, slowly and hesitatingly and
wondering why she was getting up as if she intended to
leave. Not knowing it was the old trick of bringing the
customer down, causing the hunger. At the same time
letting him see the rest of it, from the breasts on down
to the ankles. The glossy tightness of yellow velvet pressed

against a juicy hip, and going around in back where the bulge was just right, not too big and sure as hell not too small.

But of course she wasn't leaving. Merely going to the machine that sold chewing gum. As she put in the coin, she turned her head slightly to smile at the empty glass. Then the chin came up and she was smiling sweetly at Darby.

He took off the raglan, laid it on a chair, and sat down at the table. He looked up and watched the way she placed a stick of gum on her tongue, rolled it slowly into her mouth, rolling all the curves as she glided toward the table.

She sat down and said nothing. Just looked at the empty glass.

A waiter came over, scratching the back of his neck. At the bar, someone let out a loud laugh that rose to a shriek and stayed there. Others joined in and it was suddenly very noisy at the bar.

Through the noise, she said distinctly, as if the waiter didn't know, "I'll have a double rye." She named the brand, bonded. "With ginger ale."

"Mix it?" the waiter asked.

"Yes," she said. "Mix it."

"And you, sir?"

"The same." Mechanically.

The waiter went away. She was looking at Darby's cigarette, and he took out the pack, lit one for her, saw the way she inhaled the smoke and let it out through her nose. A performance.

Then not looking at him, as though she were consulting with herself, she said, "I don't know, it could be the heat."

"The heat?"

She smiled thickly, lazily. She took the ball of gum from her mouth and put it in the ash tray. "They all say that mister. Pretending they don't know what the heat means."

"I don't know what it means."

Her eyes made a casual study of the white collar, the

salt-and-pepper suit. "Maybe you don't." And the smile dimmed. "The heat," she explained, "is the law. You know what the law is?"

"They tell me it's City Hall."

"That's it, George."

"Why George?"

"You look square."

"I am." He stared at the ash tray. "Just a square named George."

"I'm Terry."

He stared at the ash tray. "Hello, Terry."

She worked on the cigarette for some moments, then said, "I'm built nice, ain't I?"

He nodded.

"You want some?"

Before he could reply, the waiter came with the drinks, At the bar the noise had lessened, and some of them were saying good night to Maxie. Darby paid for the drinks and remained quiet until the waiter was back there ducking underneath the bar. Then he said, "Where do we go?"

But she was busy with the drink. The drink was better than anything else in this world, and therefore more important. She kept the glass to her lips until it was half emptied, rolled her tongue along her lips, and murmured, "It's so good."

She said it again, with the soft purring, as if her head were on a pillow, and the room was warm, and the lazy tones of saxophones mixed with the smoke of incense. With blue bulbs in the lamp and no hands on the clock.

She lowered the glass, smiled at it, lifted it again, and drained it empty.

"Want mine?" Darby offered.

Abruptly her eyes narrowed. Her mood was technical and she slanted her head to size him up from another angle.

"Say, listen," she said. "You sure you ain't the Vice Squad?"

He shrugged. "I couldn't prove it either way."

"Well, I'm sorry. I can't take chances." But she took

his drink, all the same. She finished it in three smooth gulps and set the glass on the table.

Darby leaned toward the chair where the raglan was folded.

"Wait a second." She was tapping her chin, trying to make up her mind. Then finally, "Come on, this girl likes your looks. We'll take a chance."

He helped her into a dyed muskrat and put on his raglan and they walked out.

They walked east to Franklin Square and she told him her room was not far away and they wouldn't need a taxi. They followed the row of dark red rooming houses going north along Franklin Square, then walked up a couple of short blocks and down a very narrow street, more like an alley. They went through a door that needed no key and up a flight of stairs and down a hall that had no color and hardly any light.

She took him into a room that didn't seem to belong to this shabby house. It had been an old-fashioned, high-ceilinged room, but she had known what to do with it, with a lot of mirrors and tall furniture and framed prints hanging high on solid-color walls. The bed was strictly special, super-long and super-wide, with a yellow satin quilt that reached over the sides and touched the thick, creamy rug.

"Get comfortable," she said. "I'll only be a minute."

She opened a door that led to the bathroom. She let the door stay open just an inch or so, the sound of the faucet coming through. Just a mild assurance so the man would know she used soap and water.

She was taking much longer than a minute, but he didn't mind the waiting. He sat facing the window that looked out through a gap between four-story houses and saw the snow on roofs of smaller houses. And somehow he could see all the sleepers underneath the snow-weighted roofs, as though the snow were a blanket for each and every one of them. The January blanket that kept them protected, even while it chilled them. For winter was the best time of the year, the time of chill and freezing. Winter was the big icebox that kept them from de-

cay and made everything fresh and keen and clear. Like
the cold, clear thoughts that were coming now. Because
after all, he'd be paying for it and he had a right to get
what he paid for. No matter what it was.

Coming out of the bathroom she wore a robe of white
towel material, belted fairly tightly so it swirled out from
the waist. She walked past him, loosened the belt, took
the robe off very slowly, and displayed the dark blue of
a lace-trimmed slip.

"How long you want to stay?" she asked.

He didn't say anything. He had his wallet out and
then he was putting a ten and two fives on the satin
quilt.

Instinctively she reached for the money, folded it, and
shaped it into a neat little green rectangle that she
smoothed between her fingers. But her eyes stayed on
the man.

"All right," she said. "What do you want me to do?"

She didn't like the way he was sitting there, making no
move to get undressed. She didn't like the way he said,
"I just want to look at you."

Well, there were all kinds of customers, and each had
his own way of working up to it. When they were willing
to pay twenty dollars, she was willing to give them any
treat they craved. Within reason, of course.

"Just look at me?" Her voice carried an odd little quiver that made her wonder why it was there.

He nodded.

And she said, "Then what? After you look at me, then
what?"

He didn't reply. His eyes had climbed up and away
from her eyes and he was looking at her hair, the soft
fluffy mass of her platinum-blonde hair.

His eyes were attached to her hair, and the moments
went on like that and became shadowed moments, the
quiet starting to get on her nerves, the stillness a hollow
tube until the worry flowed through and she wondered
what the wind-up would be.

"My God," she said, and tried to turn away. But the
eyes of the man had captured the platinum-blonde hair

and refused to let it loose. She had a feeling that her hair was wrapped around his eyes and tied there and she couldn't move.

Sure, there were all kinds of customers. She sold them the relief no doctor could sell, and let them walk out and down the street like any other solid citizen.

But this one, this one here, he was scaring her. He sat there looking at her platinum-blonde hair as though the fluffy, silky softness was the only thing in the world he needed to see. As though she'd damn well better stand here and let him see it, or something terrible would happen.

So it went on like that, on and on, and finally she couldn't take it any longer, and she said, "Hey, what the hell's wrong with you?"

She knew he didn't hear.

"Come on," she said. "Come on, the party's over."

But he didn't hear.

"Now look, mister." She moved in and reached out to shake his shoulder. But she didn't need to touch him, because just then he came out of the fog, or the deep pool, or whatever it was, and got up from the chair.

He was working his way into the sleeves of the raglan.

"You mean it?" Her lips hardly moved. "You really going?" Calling herself a sap for saying anything. Just let him get out of here, and the sooner the better. No two ways about it, this one gave her the creeps.

He was at the door. "Good night, Terry."

His eyes were unsmiling, but they held a vast tenderness, a tenderness that floated there, taking her away and away through time, all the way back to the long-ago time when she'd been in love with a boy and it was going to last forever.

His hand was on the knob, but she said, "Wait," and wondered what else there was to say. Then she frowned at the folded money in her hand. "Twenty dollars he pays. Just to look at me."

"Good night."

"But wait." She looked down at the dark blue lace of her fancy slip. "Even your eyes, they stayed upstairs. I didn't even have to get undressed." She lifted her hand to the platinum-blonde curls. "You were looking at this."

He gazed past her, toward the window and beyond the window. And he nodded.

She lowered the hand and put it on her hip. Her head slanted. "Is that the way it is with you? Is that the way you get your kicks?"

"No." He spoke to something far out there past the window.

And she believed him. So there was nothing else to say except good night, nothing else to do but lock the door after he walked out.

Well, there were all kinds.

Chapter 7

His mind was vacant now, and the only thing he knew was that he didn't care. He walked through the pitch-black chasm of somewhere past five in the morning, his coat unbuttoned, the muffler missing, the snow inside his shoes and melting there, but no awareness of it, no feeling.

He went south on Eighth Street all the way down to Locust, then west on Locust, not knowing it was Locust. The wind came blasting westward from the ocean, picked up more cold from the ice on the river, hacked away at his head and shoulders, and tried to cut through his knees. It went on trying until finally it knocked him down, hurling him off the pavement, sending him head-first into the hill of hard snow banked along the curb.

He didn't mind it in the least. He just stayed there with all the jagged edges biting at his hands and wrists. He figured it was an all-right place to take a nap. But then he moved his wrist and the dial of the wrist watch said five-twenty. Soon they'd be cleaning the streets and they'd find him here and it would be embarrassing.

As he lifted himself from the snow he saw the hotel across the street and decided he could use a mattress for a few hours. He went into the hotel and told the clerk to wake him up at eight. The elevator took him to the ninth floor and he gave the boy a quarter, waited for the boy to leave, and then made three slow struggling steps to the bed and fell on it and was asleep.

At eight the phone rang and he lifted it off the hook and said thanks. Then he lowered the phone and put his legs over the side of the bed and sat there for the better part of a minute, until the phone displayed itself with a certain urgency and he picked it up again and called his house.

Vivian said hello and he told her who was calling and then there was a long pause.

She asked him where he was calling from, and he told her.

Then there was another long pause.

He leaned back from the mouthpiece and looked at it and grinned at it.

It was as though she could see the grin. She said, "I hope you're having fun."

He stopped grinning. "Aren't you worried that I didn't come home last night?"

Then it was almost as though she could see into his brain. "No. And you don't like that, do you? You want me to be worried."

He didn't say anything. Just frowned at the telephone. Then he heard her saying, "Better let me talk to her."

"Who?"

"The woman."

"Don't talk crazy," he said. "I'm here alone."

"Really? What time did she leave?"

He didn't reply.

"All right," Vivian said. Then casually, "Will you be home tonight?"

"Sure."

"All right."

He waited a few moments, but there was nothing else. He pictured her sitting there in the breakfast nook, waiting for him to hang up. He hung up, and then the smile came back and his eyes narrowed as he counted very slowly to fifteen, lifted the phone again, and called his house.

The line was busy.

He let out a little laugh that sounded almost merry.

In the lobby he smoked a cigarette, glanced at the front page of the Inquirer, then went down to the barbershop and had a shave. He went into the coffee shop with a good appetite and had orange juice and ham and eggs and read Webster's opinion of a young colored welterweight who looked ready to mix with the best of them. He read Sullivan and Winchell until it was eight-fifty-five; it was just about a ten-minute walk from here to the office.

At Ninth and Chestnut, just as he reached the corner, the street turned upside down.

He leaned against a pole, his eyes closed. A dozen hammers, all shaped like question marks, banged away at him and became twenty-four hammers and went on multiplying. There were too many questions. But all at once they merged and became a single question that had nothing to do with anyone except himself.

It was the business concerning the platinum-blonde hair. He remembered it now, exactly the way it had happened. Each move, each gesture, down to the smallest detail. He had paid twenty dollars just to sit there and look at the platinum-blonde hair.

Not knowing why. Knowing only the externals of the episode. Not knowing what had been in his mind as he sat there and looked. Knowing and not knowing and the street was upside down.

He said to himself, If her hair had been any other color, I wouldn't have given it a second glance.

And he remembered yesterday, during lunch with Harry, when it had appeared that the waitress, Miss Dennis, had platinum-blonde hair.

He went back two nights to the darkness of the bedroom, and Vivian's hair changing color, from dark brown to platinum blonde.

His mind leaped back to now, right now. A woman was crossing the street and coming toward him. A woman wearing a beaver coat. Whose hair was platinum blonde.

The woman passed him, and he didn't turn, just stood there leaning against the pole and saying to himself, Go on, follow her. Go on, idiot, get yourself arrested.

He decided it was just a little too much for him to handle alone.

At lunchtime he sat with Harry Clawson in a sea-food house that had white tile walls and white-topped tables. The waiters wore yachting caps and there were anchors and life preservers and boathooks all over the place.

"In other words," Harry said, "they want us to know they sell fish."

"What are you having?"

"Oysters," Harry replied. "A dozen raw, to start."

"To start what?" He smiled dimly, referring to the old theory about oysters.

"I wonder if it's true," Harry mused.

"If it is, I could use two dozen."

And wasn't sorry he had said it. He needed Harry's help. He felt the trembling urgency of needing help and told himself it couldn't wait. He had to get straightened out on this platinum-blonde issue. He had to have it answered and settled before he settled the other issue.

The waiter was there, taking the order, telling Harry they'd run out of shrimp creole but he could follow the oysters with red snapper. Harry said that was fine. The waiter walked away.

Harry grinned, picking it up where they'd left off. "Don't worry about it. It's like an automobile. In the wintertime it freezes up."

Darby shrugged, toying with a spoon. "Oh, well. I guess it's always comical when it happens to someone else."

The grin stayed, but Harry's tone was consoling. "Don't take it so serious. Maybe all you need is vitamins."

"I wonder."

Harry put the grin aside. "Say, boy," and his eyes were the eyes of a close friend, genuinely concerned. "You sound like you're having real trouble."

Darby nodded. He wondered if it was possible to discuss this matter without referring to the other matter.

Harry was quiet, waiting tactfully.

"I found out last night," Darby said. "Felt restless. Vivian went to bed early and I went out for a walk."

"In all that cold?"

"Took a taxi downtown and went into a bar. And I saw a woman."

Harry looked up at the ceiling.

"A professional," Darby said. "She took me to her room."

It caught Harry off balance. "You? You went with a whore?"

"Gave her twenty dollars."

Harry glanced around aimlessly, sort of helplessly. He took the brier from his lapel pocket and rubbed the bowl for no reason at all and put the pipe back in.

"I didn't do anything," Darby said.

"All right, let's try that again. You paid her twenty dollars and you didn't do anything."

"Just sat there and looked at her. Then I walked out."

The waiter came with the food and put the plates on the table and moved away. Harry caught an oyster on his fork and flipped it into his mouth and reached for a cracker. There was a bowl of chowder in front of Darby but he paid it no attention.

He said, "Well? What do you think?"

But Harry was concentrating on the oyster. After he had it down he hooked another oyster and dipped it in the red sauce. Presently he said, "I'll tell you what I think. I think you're a damn fool to let it bother you."

"But I didn't even touch her."

"Of course you didn't. Go on, eat your soup."

"I'm trying to figure—"

"There's nothing to figure. It's as easy as adding one and one. She gives you the come-on and you think you're excited. She gets undressed and you give her the twenty, but then you're stopped cold."

"Why?"

Wearily, "Come on, boy, come on." Then louder, as though it was the only possible answer, "Vivian. That's why."

"No."

It was an emphatic no, and it pulled the rein on Harry and drew him to a stiff halt.

Darby gazed dully at the edge of the table. "She was a platinum blonde."

"What?"

"Platinum blonde."

"So?"

"That's all I wanted to do. Just look at it."

Harry grimaced impatiently. "Look at what?"

"All that silk on her head. That fluffy platinum silk."

Then it was quiet. And after that the only sound was the clink of Harry's fork against the oyster shell. Harry tapped the shell as though the fork were a pencil and he were thoughtfully tapping it against a desktop.

Finally Harry looked up. "Al," he said, "I'm going to tell you something. Maybe you won't like it."

"Let's find out," he said with a sort of cold challenge, with a sudden hostility toward Harry and toward everyone. He was blazing angry at himself for having started this discussion.

Harry's face was solemn. "Something's come over you. You're changed. I started to notice it weeks ago. At first I didn't pay much attention. But yesterday—"

"What about yesterday?" As though he had a spear in his hand, daring the enemy to come closer.

"At lunch," Harry said. "With that waitress, Miss What's-her-name—"

"Dennis." And the spear quivered. "Miss Dennis."

"The way you looked at her—"

"At her hair," he murmured aloud to himself. "The soft, silky platinum blonde."

"Al, for God's sake!" Harry hit his fist on the table. "She wasn't a platinum blonde."

The fist hit the table again but Darby didn't hear. He was somewhere way up high, much higher than the highest building on Chestnut Street. Where the air was soft and warm and sweet. Where everything was gentle and there was no trouble, no grief. Where nothing mattered.

"Now look, boy—"

He came down fast, all the way down on the steeply angled sliding board, to feel the floor under his feet, to see the plates and the spoons and the strange eyes that looked at him from the other side of the table.

He put the needle on the record and heard the mechanical voice saying, "Come on, Harry. Let's eat our lunch. It's getting late."

He dropped the spear and picked up a knife.

He smiled fondly at the blade.

Chapter 8

THEY RETURNED to the office at ten of two, and he sat down at his desk, lit a cigarette, and looked at a sheet of yellow paper filled with scribbled mathematics. It was only a matter of moments before the numbers and symbols would take on meaning and he would be able to resume work. He puffed at the cigarette and waited calmly for all the segments to get lined up on the yellow paper.

An hour later the pencil remained untouched and the yellow paper was a platter made of yellow glass. Beneath the glass a fleet of little white boats had gone down under the guns of an unseen armada, and there they were, quiet on the bottom of the placid lake. He bit at a thumbnail and took the yellow paper off the glass ash tray filled with cigarette stubs. Looked at the paper from another angle, as though that would help to clarify what was on it. But there was no clarification. The paper told him it had nothing to offer.

The desk became a smaller desk, in a classroom at Birney Grammar School. He was in the sixth grade and it was another dismal Friday when they were having the weekly arithmetic tests. It wasn't that he didn't know his arithmetic. Actually it was his favorite subject and he was one of the best in the class. But although he knew the answers, he never liked the Friday tests. It was always so quiet in the classroom, such a gloomy quiet as they bent over their papers, and he felt sorry for the dumb ones who didn't know what to do, who stared out the window or scratched their heads or bit futilely at their pencils.

On this particular Friday the arithmetic test was multiplication and long division, and as the teacher said,

"All right, start now," he began copying the problems
from the blackboard and went at it unhurriedly until
the yellow paper contained all the problems and all he
had to do was multiply and divide and get his gold star
for a perfect score. But all at once there was nothing
on the paper.

And he stared across the room, at the thick neck of
a boy named Newton, who had dared him, during recess,
to fight after school. He hadn't said yes or no to the dare,
and Newton made it more emphatic by punching him
in the mouth. Before he could answer that, the bell had
rung to end recess. So now he had to fight Newton after
school, and all the other boys in the class knew about it.
They'd all be there, in the empty lot over on Seventh
Street, and they'd stand in a circle and watch him getting
his head knocked off by Newton Colton, the toughest kid
in the fifth grade.

When the bell rang to end the period he handed in his
paper with all the spaces empty where the answers ought
to be. And he didn't care. He saw Newton turning to leer
at him with thin lips, and a thick fist moving back and
forth to let him know he was in for it.

Tons of fear were crushing his chest, and cotton was
packed tightly far down in his throat. The sound of the
final bell ended the school day, and he began the slow
death march up to the lot on Seventh Street, where he
got the black eye that he'd known all along he would get.
And the bloody nose. He got his face all banged up
before they stopped it and he walked home alone, trying
with all his might not to cry as he entered the house.

He entered through the back door and saw his sister
Marjorie in the kitchen. She stared at his battered face.
Then she took out her handkerchief and wiped the blood
from his nose and mouth. He felt so much better now that
he was here with Marjorie. She was so wonderful, she
took all the pain away as she put her arms around him
and kissed his bruised forehead. Not like an older sister
at all, because the kiss sent a strange warm shiver running down and up and down again, all through his insides. He wondered if his lips would have the same effect

on Marjorie. He wanted to give her this same marvelous feeling that she was giving him, and he kissed her on the cheek. And then something happened, something that he couldn't understand. He didn't know who caused it, or what caused it, but somehow his lips were on Marjorie's lips. He tasted the delightful flavor of her mouth and it was like riding on a carrousel with his eyes closed and getting dizzy but not wanting the ride to end. He held her very tightly and it was impossible to let go and the carrousel went around and around.

And he heard Marjorie whispering, "Hold me tighter."

It was so easy to obey the gentle command of the princess.

"Oh," Marjorie moaned. "Oh, what are you doing?"

There was no way to answer that. He really had no idea what he was doing, except that he was going around and around and up and up, and the world was very far away.

"You little devil," Marjorie whispered. "Stop doing that."

But he couldn't stop. And he knew she didn't want him to stop.

He shut his eyes tightly and tried with all his might to understand what was happening. But there was no way to understand it. The feeling was so different, so queer, and completely separated from anything else he had ever felt. He sort of sensed that he and Marjorie were doing something they shouldn't do, and yet it didn't seem like something bad. Not at all like saying dirty words, or writing things on the walls of the boys' room. Not at all like the time when the family went to Uncle Ted's place in the country and he sneaked into the barn with his Cousin Harriet and they played a game called Doctors and Nurses. This wasn't anything like that. This was something very big and important, because Marjorie was his favorite person, and he'd do anything for Marjorie, he'd go out and fight a grizzly bear if she asked him to. He knew she meant more to him than anyone else in the entire universe, and that included his mother and father. Just thinking about it made his eyes wet.

And Marjorie whispered, "Why, Alvin. You're crying."
He shook his head.

"But you are." Her voice was so soft, so gentle, and just to see her face so near was the greatest gift he could ever hope for.

Yet the only way he could put it in words was: "I'm so glad you're my sister."

Her hands were velvet on his face. "You like me a lot?"

"More than anything. Up to the sky and down again."

"That much?"

"Yes," he said. "And more than that." He tried to blink the tears away. "Do you like me?"

Her eyes came closer. "I'll tell you a secret. You're my best boy friend."

He couldn't feel the floor under his feet. It really seemed as if he was floating. And then, desperately, he took hold of her wrists. "Make me a promise. Tell me you'll never go away."

Her face was solemn. "I can't promise that."

He swallowed hard. "Why not?"

"Well," she said, "someday I'll grow up and I'll be a woman. And then I'll get married."

"And what about me?"

"You'll get married, too."

"No," he said.

"But you will," she mildly insisted. "Everybody gets married."

"Not me," and his mouth was set stubbornly. "I won't ever get married. Unless," and his eyes widened at the thought, "unless I marry you."

Her smile was sad. "You know we can't do that."

"Why can't we?"

"I'm your sister. You can't marry your own sister."

"But why? What's to stop us? Is there a law against it?"

"Of course," she said. "Of course there is. Didn't you know that?"

He didn't reply. He felt heavy and choked, and after some moments he said, despairingly, "I know what'll happen. You'll get married and go away and I'll never see you any more."

"Don't say that. We'll see each other."

He sighed heavily. "No, we won't. You'll do what Mother did. She left Seattle and never went back. We got uncles there we've never seen."

Marjorie turned very slowly, as though she couldn't bear the sight of his anguish. Then, her head lowered, she said, "No matter where I go, no matter how far away, I'll always come back to you."

His eyes began to brighten. "You mean that?"

She faced him. "I swear it."

And again she put her arms around him and kissed him, and once more he was in the land of enchantment where the carrousel went around and around, with the warmth of Marjorie's arms and the cool sweetness of her lips.

And the wondrous light in her pale green eyes.

The glowing treasure of her long and wavy hair. Platinum blonde.

He sat there at the desk in the insurance office nine stories above Chestnut Street with his knuckles pressed against his eyes, with the hammers banging away deep inside as he told himself that the color of his sister's hair was not platinum blonde, but dark brown. Then he told himself he was wrong, it was platinum blonde. But no, it was dark brown. Then no again. Platinum blonde.

He begged himself to stop it, and realized that the only way to stop it was to figure it out. He decided it shouldn't be too difficult. Just a process of remembering.

At that moment a hand fell on his shoulder. He looked up and saw Harry Clawson.

"Now look," Harry said firmly. "You've got to come out of it. I've been watching you. You're sitting here all tied up in knots."

He pointed to the yellow paper. "I've got a tough one here."

Harry leaned over and scanned the paper. "Tough? You know this isn't tough. It's strictly elementary. You're wracking your brains with that other problem. That platinum-blonde business."

He wished Harry would go away.

Harry pulled a chair to the side of the desk and sat down. There was a clumsy quiet while they stared at each other.

Suddenly Harry snapped his fingers. "I think I've got the answer."

He grimaced wearily. "Look, I have work to do. It's a quarter to four."

"No, it isn't." Harry's smile was thin and clinical. "It's right around midnight."

"What the hell are you talking about?"

"Midnight," Harry said. "Six years ago. A Thanksgiving dance. You were stag that night." He leaned forward. "My date was a platinum blonde."

Darby picked up a book of matches. He looked at the advertisement that claimed this candy bar was really something different.

"Remember?" Harry was leaning forward.

"No."

"Pale green eyes. A page-boy bob. Built slim and streamlined."

He stared down at the book of matches. "Something really different."

"You bet your sweet life she was different. The looks were phenomenal. The personality was pure poison. First and last time I ever took her out."

He shook his head. "I don't remember."

"You don't?" And Harry tightened the smile. "The hell you don't." The smile faded and the words came out slowly. "Her name was Geraldine."

Darby dropped the book of matches. He reached down to pick it up and his arm became a bar of cold metal that he couldn't move.

Harry's voice was far away. "Geraldine Barrett."

Along the curving tracks of Darby's brain the name was a lit fuse running wild. Somewhere near the center of his brain the powder exploded and he had no idea where he was.

"Now," Harry said. "Do you remember?"

But now Harry wasn't there.

Until Harry had hold of his arm, the fingers pressing tightly so that it hurt.

"All right," Harry said. "Snap out of it."

Darby picked up the book of matches and smiled at the cover as though it were someone's face. "Geraldine Barrett."

"You see now?" Harry's eyes were keen. "You understand?"

He nodded.

"As simple as that," and once more Harry snapped his fingers. "The only platinum blonde you ever knew. The only real trouble you ever had. Remember the nights we sat up and talked about it? Until four, five in the morning. And it didn't matter, because you couldn't sleep anyway."

It seemed that everything was adding up, but it was happening too fast and he wanted a closer look at it. "That was six years ago."

"So what? It came back, that's all. It just opened the door and walked in."

"Why didn't I realize?"

Harry tapped the back of his head. "Here's where it was. You just couldn't see it."

"I'm not sure I see it now."

"Take your time," Harry advised. "Think about it. Remember it the way it happened. Just straighten it out and clear it up."

He struck a match and looked at the flame.

Harry said, "It's easy, boy. You'll see how easy it is. I'll let you take it from here." He got up, patted Darby's shoulder, and walked away.

So that now, as Darby looked down at the yellow paper, it became the shiny yellow floor of the dance hall, and it was Thanksgiving Eve six years ago. It was a formal dance, and he stood among the stags wearing a $19.95 tuxedo. The other stags were moving out upon the floor to cut in, but he didn't see them, he didn't see any of the evening gowns and silver slippers. Except the black and silver worn by the platinum blonde who had her eyes on him as she danced with Harry.

Her pale green eyes. And her silver-yellow page-boy bob. He wondered where Harry had found her, and wondered why he felt just a little sorry for Harry. Then he knew the reason as Harry danced her close to him and he got a careful look at the pale green eyes. He knew she was trouble, real trouble, a first-class tease artist if he'd ever seen one. The way she floated in toward Harry so that Harry was encouraged and held her more tightly. The way she pulled back and looked at Harry slantwise as though to ask him what he thought he was doing. The orchestra played on and Darby stood there looking at her.

Finally Harry brought her over and they were introduced. "This is Geraldine." The lips smiled just a little and the pale green eyes didn't smile at all, just worked their way into him. He heard the music playing and asked Harry if it was all right. Why, sure, Harry said, but Geraldine said no, she felt like sitting it out, and told Harry to get her a glass of punch.

She gave Darby her phone number and told him to call her up tomorrow. At ten, she said. Ten sharp. Not a minute later, because she'd be gone.

Just for a laugh, he told himself. Just to see what happens here. And he phoned, the next day, at five after ten. He heard the phone ringing, let it ring for a minute, and put it back on the hook, the frown starting on his brow, the frown deeper on Friday when he phoned for a date and she turned him down. He made his confession to Harry, and Harry laughed. Don't be a fool, Harry said. Forget it, it's grief. It's grief in spades.

But he phoned again. Three and four times. Six and seven times. And heard the calm no, not rude at all, just no. But the tone of it told him to keep on trying, and finally one night she told him to come on over.

She lived in the Kensington section, near Allegheny Avenue. She and her brother were partners in a small business enterprise, a candy shop. He fully expected she'd keep him waiting at least thirty minutes, but when he arrived he saw her sitting there with her coat on, looking at her watch.

Calmly she told him he was four minutes late. He grinned and she asked him what was funny, and he wondered aloud if she'd ever had a job with the railroad. She said she didn't think that was very funny. It was important, she said, that people keep their appointments on time. He said he couldn't argue with that, and heard himself apologizing for being four minutes late.

She accepted the apology and he took her to the movies, drove his Ford through the black-green lanes of Roosevelt Boulevard, went all the way out to Langhorne, then past Langhorne toward Trenton, with the radio going and Woody Herman playing the clarinet, until Geraldine told him to turn off the music and turn off the road and park somewhere.

The Ford coasted down a narrow lane, then off that and into a clearing with trees very high and thick all around. He cut the engine and put his arm around her shoulders. She let that happen and let him come in close, but as his lips approached her mouth she put her thumb on his chin and pushed him away. He told himself to play it cool, and then, just as he shrugged, she had the same thumb going inside his shirt, the thumbnail cutting his chest, the nail moving slowly but somehow like a razor blade as it went around in a three-quarter circle, came up straight, then cut in at right angles. Engraving a red G on his chest.

She told him what it was, a G, for Geraldine. And told him to start the car and take her home.

He took her home and tried to kiss her good night and knew she'd say no. But he had to try. He had to call her the next day. He had to find out why he couldn't throw her out of his mind, and why it wasn't easy to fall asleep. But especially he had to find out why the red G on his chest wouldn't stop burning.

Night after night he went on seeing Geraldine. Every night in the week it was Geraldine. She wouldn't let him kiss her and eventually he quit trying to kiss her and tried instead, in several little ways, to irritate her. He came late, he came unshaved, he came once and said he didn't have a dime in his pockets and they'd just have to take a walk. And all she did was smile right through him, pick up his strategy and look at it and drop it with a shrug; let him know the G was on his chest and he couldn't get it off.

It went on like that for almost a month. He stopped trying to irritate her, stopped trying to fight the thing, knowing somehow there was no way to fight it. He phoned three and four and five times a day. And there were days when he couldn't work at all and he'd go up to Kensington and hang around the candy shop, and her brother would grin at him as though he was just another fool in a long line of fools.

Winter was gray and mean upon the city and every night was a package of cold bleak hours, like the hours in a cell that had no door.

Then one night he brought her home from a cabaret where he'd spent much more than he could afford. She told him to come on in, she wanted to see something. They went into the parlor at the rear of the shop and she unbuttoned his shirt and took a look at his chest. The red G was gone and there was no scar, nothing. She said it was time for him to be branded again.

He told her to go to hell. He turned and started to walk out and she had his arm, causing him to pivot and come back and get the full thrust of her body, her hands catching hold of his face and everything on fire as her lips parted and they breathed the air in each other's mouth.

It was very fast, that first time. They were on the couch, and then they were off the couch and it was all over. It was like jumping out the window and landing on the street. A quick ride, just like that.

On the following night she wouldn't let him kiss her. For the better part of a week she wouldn't let him kiss her, wouldn't even let him hold her hand. When he asked her what was wrong, she only shrugged and said she wasn't in the mood. He became very angry and started to shout and she said it was a pity he couldn't control his temper and perhaps he'd better take her home. He said all right, goddamnit, and he took her home and drove three blocks, went into a drugstore, called her and begged her to forgive him. She told him to come on back, hurry back, and he drove back. The door was open. He ran in. And there she was on the couch, waiting for him.

And again the next night, with the platinum-blonde hair flowing onto her shoulders and the pale green eyes half closed, sending the weird green flame onto his bared chest, branding him with a G that had no line, no color, but was engraved deeply nonetheless, so that he could feel the G scorching him deep inside.

Then all the nights continuing in a timeless path where there was only the green flame, the silver-yellow of her hair dripping over the edge of the couch, dangling over the dark floor that didn't seem to be a floor at all, just a dark emptiness.

He bought her things. He bought perfume and boxes of candy. He bought nylon stockings and a handbag and a cigarette lighter. She said thank you, Alvin, and maybe an hour later she was mentioning casually that it would be nice if she had a topaz ring.

He bought her a topaz ring. He was spending all his money, taking her to restaurants where dinner cost four and a half. She didn't even look at the menu. First, she said, she'd have a Daiquiri, and then she'd have sirloin steak. It was always a Daiquiri and then sirloin steak. Why, for God's sake, he was making less than forty a week and spending eighty and ninety. He was racing through his bank roll and he couldn't let it go on like this, he just couldn't.

But it went on. And day by day it became more expensive. She needed some dental work and he footed the bill for that. Her brother got drunk on a Saturday night and fell in the street and broke his ankle, and all she did was display the doctor's bill. So he paid for that, too. It moved toward the point where he was paying for almost everything.

It reached that point and passed it. He took out a loan on his car, then couldn't pay off on the loan, and went to Harry. He listened as Harry labeled him an idiot,

a maniac, just listened but didn't really pay attention.
He just said he needed fifty. Harry gave him the fifty
and begged him to break it off, break it off now, call her
up and tell her it was ended.

He said no, he couldn't do that. But that was when
he began to have the late-at-night discussions with Harry, heading sort of frantically toward Harry's house after
he said good night to Geraldine. He and Harry would
sit in the Ford, with cigarette butts all over the floor
boards and the glow of a street lamp coming through
the windshield.

And the springtime night was soft and sweet, the dark
windows were gentle velvet curtains, guarding the bliss
of all the married couples who slept in each other's arms.

Harry begged him to get rid of her, find himself a nice
girl who would make him happy. Sure, he ought to get
married to a nice girl. There was plenty of nice girls,
Harry said. And he added, almost as though the deci-
sion had been made in that instant, that he'd soon be
popping the question to Gertrude Warren. But this
Geraldine, this sure as hell wasn't marriage material. It
was trouble, it was grief.

Then it was the middle of April and four-thirty in the
morning when Harry's words really hit home. Harry
was turning down his request for another loan. He owed
Harry almost three hundred dollars and his other debts
amounted to four hundred more. Harry told him if he
had an ounce of brains, an ounce of self-respect, he'd
go to the nearest phone and tell her it was all over.

Harry stayed with him as he drove to an all-night
gas station. He called the number and there was no answer. That didn't make sense; he'd said good night to
her only a couple of hours ago. He told Harry he couldn't
understand it, and he'd better go there right away in case
something was wrong. Harry muttered that he ought to
get his head kicked in, she was probably lifting glasses
in an after-hour joint. He didn't have time to get sore at
Harry's remark. He was alone in the Ford, facing toward
Kensington.

He parked outside the candy shop, waiting there until

past six, when the taxi drove up and she got out and ran to him. She told him she'd just come from the hospital. Her brother had been seized with a heart attack and she doubted that he'd live through the week.

Three days later her brother died. She said there wasn't enough money for the funeral expenses, her brother had drunk up what little money there was. It was sort of tough, she murmured, when there weren't any parents and none of the relatives were any good, none of them gave a damn.

He went out and borrowed more money and paid for the funeral. They were in the Ford, driving away from the cemetery, and Geraldine began to wonder aloud what to do now and where to go.

He stopped the car. He put his arms around her. He told himself it would be all right, as he told Geraldine they'd get married.

But he realized, within a week, that it was going to be difficult, really rough. He was practically living there with her in Kensington, and he discovered that living with her was sheer torture. No matter what he did, it was absolutely impossible to please her. She had the venomous habit of starting an argument and refusing to hear his side of it. Then later, in bed, when he was sure the argument was forgotten, and he'd move toward her, she'd edge away from him. Ever so slightly.

Causing him to grit his teeth as though he were being torn apart.

Toward the end of that week he was eating a skimpy lunch, seated at the counter of a little place on Sixth, off Chestnut, when he spotted Harry Clawson. He caught Harry's eye, and Harry came in and ordered a cup of coffee. Harry insisted that he come to the engagement party. It was tonight, Harry reminded him, and he must come.

He wanted to know if Geraldine was invited.

All right, Harry said. Geraldine was invited.

After work, when he returned to the rooms in Kensington, she wasn't there. He saw a note, telling him she had to go somewhere and wouldn't be back until late. It was the kind of note she'd have left for the milk-man, but it didn't annoy him. He sensed a certain relief in knowing that she wasn't here and he could go to the party without her.

He went to Harry's engagement party and grinned as he congratulated Gertrude. An easy grin, the first easy grin he'd worn for a long time. It was a nice party and it was really swell to be with the old crowd again.

Then it was past eleven and he wondered if Geraldine was home yet. He was moving toward the phone when someone tugged at his arm and urged him across the room and introduced him to a girl named Vivian.

At three that morning Geraldine hurled a thick glass ash tray at his head. She missed with the ash tray and tried again with a lamp. She missed with that and came at him with her fingernails aimed for his eyes. He caught hold of her wrists and begged her to listen. He said she mustn't blame him, she mustn't hate him, it just had to happen, that was all. He was sorry he had taken up her time, but that was part of the game, it was a chance they'd both have to take.

He said it was simply a matter of finding out whether he could go through with it. And he couldn't go through with it. If he played it noble and true blue, and married her, it would be a terrible mistake for both of them, be-cause no matter what efforts were made, they wouldn't stay married. Sooner or later he'd walk out. Or she would walk out. They just weren't suited to each other. It was as simple as that.

No, she said, it wasn't as simple as that. She warned him, if he walked out, he'd be sorry as long as he lived.

She cried to him, as he moved toward the door, "Don't leave me, Alvin. Please don't. Please."

She cursed him as he reached the door. She ran toward him and staggered and fell, screaming curses at him.

But as he opened the door the screaming was ended and her voice was somber and hollow, saying, "You'll come back. Someday, I know it, you'll come back."

The April breeze said it again and again as he hur-ried away from Kensington.

Chapter 9

His HEAD was bent low over the desktop and his eyes were closed. There was no feeling of being in any special place, and he might have been kneeling in an unlit cave, or seated in a smoky room where there were no faces, just a lot of eyes that looked at him. Or merely drifting on a slab of ice in a quiet region of white emptiness.

All at once he heard a blast of screaming noise that caused him to shut his eyes tighter. His brain turned a volume lever and made the noise many times louder than it actually was. So now it was the noise of a jungle on fire and all the animals going crazy.

Actually it was the noise from the mills and factories, the five-o'clock whistle. He raised his head and saw the yellow paper with all the numbers and symbols on it, saw the untouched pencil. A smile that he couldn't feel came onto his lips and he told himself it was like any other line of business. There were good days and bad days. This just happened to· be one of those afternoons when he hadn't been able to get any work done.

At all the other desks they were winding things up, putting their papers in order, making final tabulations, or simply leaning back to light a cigarette and enjoy the knowledge that it was five o'clock and they could go home. He saw Harry Clawson conferring with someone toward the rear of the room, and his eyes narrowed with wariness. Somehow, for some vague reason, it was very important that he get out of here without being seen by Harry.

There was a certain stealth in his movements as he rose from the desk, put the papers in the wire tray, glided into the aisle leading to the exit. The stealth stayed there as he entered the elevator, and his eyes remained narrow while the elevator went down nine floors to Chestnut Street.

On the street he joined the going-home crowd that moved clumsily on the icy pavement. But his own stride was smooth and relaxed, as though there were no ice, no danger of slipping. He walked up to Eighth and Market and saw the entrance to the Frankford elevated, the stairway going down underneath the street, telling him to come in and pay his fare and go home.

His face was blank as he told the Frankford elevated to wait a while, he wasn't quite ready to go home, he had some other things to do. But he had no idea what those other things were. He crossed Market Street and continued north on Eighth.

It was getting dark and the lights were on in the store windows. The lights strung themselves out in an illuminated chain that pulled him on up Eighth Street. He went up Eighth, past Arch, going toward the vari-colored lights of the tenderloin.

Then he was there in the tenderloin, seeing all the ragged coat collars turned up, all the faces stiff and cold. Some of them walked heavily, their feet bound with rags and newspaper to keep the winter from biting off the toes. They jammed the street, walking up and down with no place to go. They came out of flophouses with no good reason for coming out.

A scribbled menu was pasted to a restaurant window and announced some important changes in price quotations. The spaghetti was down five cents and the stew was down ten. The stew situation was underlined. Several pairs of watery eyes took in the stew issue, standing there on the pavement and looking at the menu with calculating interest. With the same quiet urgency as the eyes in a Wall Street brokerage, looking at an important change on the blackboard.

Darby was hungry. He went inside and sat down at the counter and told the man he wanted stew.

Farther on down the counter a voice said, "Comes out of stir and goes right back in."

And another voice asked, "What he do?"

"What he always does. Grabbed a six-year-old kid."

"They oughta burn him."

"Ain't there any cure?"

"Sure, there's a cure. Just burn him."

A third voice horned in. "You ain't got any right to talk. Who knows what you do?"

"You don't know, so shut up."

"I'll tell you what you do. You go in the men's room and draw pictures on the wall."

"So what's wrong with that?"

"Y'oughta learn how to draw. Ya make them women look like elephants."

"Well, that's the way I like 'em. Big as elephants."

Seated in the stool next to Darby, a heavy-set man wearing two sweaters leaned back and gazed reflectively at the ceiling. "Very interesting," he mused.

Darby looked at him. "What's interesting?"

"That elephant complex." And he pointed down the counter at the man who drew the pictures on lavatory walls. Darby saw that the man was short and skinny.

"You see?" The heavy-set man had the manner of a diagnostician. "The driving need to climb Mount Everest. To conquer a nation. Thus he creates the magnifying glass to increase his stature."

The stew arrived, with two chunks of white bread and a soup spoon. Darby picked up the spoon and without testing the taste of the stew he began eating it heartily, enjoying it immediately, hungry for more of it, without a thought for what its contents were.

The heavy-set man gnawed on a pig's foot. "There's a basis for everything. I'd have owned a yacht today if I hadn't stayed overnight in Mobile." He uncovered a piece of meat and ripped it off with his fingers. "Should I tell you why I stayed overnight?"

"No," Darby said. "Tell me about my complex."

The big round face turned slowly. "What is it?"

"Platinum-blonde hair."

The heavy-set man cupped his chin in his hand. "On women?" he asked, and answered it, "Well, of course."

He tapped the pig's bone against his teeth. Then he looked closer at Darby and shook his head as Darby wanted to speak. As though to tell Darby it really wasn't necessary, what had been said was sufficient.

"Actually," the heavy-set man said, "you can't stand the sight of platinum-blonde hair."

Darby beckoned to the man behind the counter. He told the man he wanted a cup of coffee, no cream.

"And actually," the heavy-set man continued, "you can't stand the taste of that stew."

"I'm eating it."

"No, you're not. You're forcing it down."

"You kidding?" Darby grinned. "It's damn good stew."

"I wouldn't get near it. And I'll tell you something. I've been eating in this dump for years. I trust them with everything but stew."

Darby shrugged easily. "Well, every man to his taste. It just happens I like it."

"It happens you hate it. Thus, the summary. For some reason, you're inflicting a penalty on yourself."

The coffee came. Darby stirred it slowly. "What reason?"

The heavy-set man leaned back on the stool and folded his arms. "I'm very much afraid that's a big problem. If we could sit here for a month we might gain an inch toward the answer."

Darby sipped the coffee. "It can't be that much trouble." He took out cigarettes. The heavy-set man accepted one and said thanks. They smoked without speaking for a little while and then Darby murmured, "Forget it. Just forget I said anything."

He got up and walked out.

But he felt the pressure of an echo against his head as he moved along up Eighth Street. The voice of the heavy-set man. It was a hammer and it had more force than the January wind racing in from the Delaware.

Then it wasn't an echo at all. The voice was actually there. He could feel the hand on his arm. He pulled away swiftly, almost with violence, and heard the heavy-set man saying, "Let's talk about it."

"Keep away." It was animal, a low growl.

"Now, don't be foolish." The heavy-set man moved in again.

"I said keep away. Mind your own goddamn business."

"Look, friend. I only want to help you."

"Who said I needed help?"

"I say it. I know it." The thick finger came up and waved a warning. "You're in bad shape."

"That's my lookout."

"Listen, friend." The heavy-set man was solemn. "The mood you're in now, you're liable to get yourself in trouble."

He backed away and regarded the heavy-set man as though the bulky shape was another adversary. As though the lit cigarette was one of the fires in the enemy camp.

He heard the voice saying, "See the way it is? You're not functioning. Something's out of line."

"Just go away. Leave me alone."

"See what I mean? That torture chamber gets uncomfortable. Your own hands shoved you in, but you say to yourself it was other hands."

"It was."

"That's bad, friend. That's very bad thinking. Now you're way out there. Better come on back in."

He thought that the man meant he was out in the street and he would get run over. His head turned to see if a car was approaching.

"Come on, friend." With a genuine desire to help, and an equal amount of curiosity. "What you need is a lift. Let's go and have a drink."

"I knew we'd get to that." He took his wallet out. He showed his teeth as he extended the dollar bill. "Go on, buy your whisky. That's what you've been after all along."

The heavy-set man didn't look at the money. His eyes were saying it was too bad, it was a pity. Futility came into his voice. "I think it's too late." Then, as though Darby wasn't there, "I think he's really crossed the railroad tracks."

Darby was concentrating on the wallet and the delicate operation of putting the bill in the wallet and putting the wallet in his pocket. He did it very slowly and carefully.

"I'll make one more try," the heavy-set man decided aloud. He took a cautious step toward the area of danger. "Stay with yourself," he urged. "Just yourself. Don't take it out on anyone else."

"Anyone else? Who, for instance?"

"That's what bothers me. I don't know who." And then the thick hand made a rapier thrust. "If I knew, I'd go and warn them."

The low growl again. "You better keep out of it."

And that was all for now. He saw the heavy-set man retreating slowly, told himself he was rid of the obstacle and he could go ahead with his plans. He turned and continued north on Eighth Street.

He turned the corner. The glowing sign read, "Pete's Cut-Rate Drugs."

He stayed on the other side of the street as he moved slowly toward the store. He stood directly across from the store and obtained a full view of what was happening inside. It was busy in there, and bright light came flooding past the green neon in the window. He counted five customers and saw Pete Lanson exhibiting a jar of something to a colored woman who had an infant in her arms.

He glanced at his wrist watch. Seven-twenty. Well, he'd just wait around until it was time for the store to close. When Mr. Lover Boy would be in there alone. He lit a cigarette and inhaled contentedly and leaned back against the brick siding of an unrented store.

He finished the cigarette and lit another.

Seven-thirty. He wondered what time the store would close. It was a neighborhood of late-hour trade and maybe the store wouldn't close until ten or eleven. It didn't make sense to just stand here and wait. And besides, it was downright foolish to let himself be seen on this street. So go on, take a walk. Go somewhere.

He tried to think of a place to go. Maybe one of the saloons. But he didn't drink and he couldn't just stand

at the bar and take up space. Of course, he could go to
a movie, but it would be warm in there and he might
fall asleep and wake up too late. Or then again, he had
some friends who lived in town and perhaps he could
pay a visit and erase two or three hours that way. . . .

But suddenly he thought that it might be nice to go
on up to Kensington. Just for old time's sake, put it that
way. After all, six years was a long time. He wondered
if she still looked the same. Harry had been right when
he'd said the looks were phenomenal. From brow to chin
the face was a white flower, strictly elegant. There were
very few faces like the face of Geraldine. And it would
sure be nice to see her again.

Just for old time's sake.

He walked over to Ninth Street and got into a taxi.

Chapter 10

GOING NORTH toward Kensington, the taxi went sliding and skidding on the slippery streets. The driver apologized for not having chains on the tires and said there'd been a jam-up at the garage this morning and someone had taken his chains. Darby said that was all right, he didn't mind. The driver said it was dangerous to drive without chains in this weather but it really wasn't his fault. He said he made it a point to give every passenger a safe ride, and he really felt bad about the chains. Darby told him not to worry about it. The taxi skidded and missed a parked truck by no more than a few inches.

Then later on, near Lehigh, the taxi skidded again and banged into a streetcar.

The driver just sat there for a moment or so, wishing he were back in the Army. The streetcar conductor had come out and had his arms bent and his fists pressed against his ribs as he approached the taxi.

People came crowding in from both sides of the street. It was always interesting when a taxi was involved. Especially when a taxi was involved with a streetcar. The people, for reasons that they never bothered to think about, were not overly friendly toward streetcar conductors and taxi drivers. They crowded in, saw there was no big damage, and were keenly disappointed.

But the streetcar conductor was vehement. He pressed his fists more tightly against his ribs and stepped back as the driver got out of the taxi. He waited while the driver looked at the streetcar's shattered light and the taxi's dented grill. And then he said, "Well, you satisfied?"

"Couldn't be helped," the driver said. "Street's like glass."

"Where the hell's your chains?"

The driver faced him. "Who you yelling at?"

"I'm yelling at you." The street car conductor pointed a long, bony finger close to the driver's eyes. "In weather like this, without chains. Where's your head?"

The driver took a deep breath.

"You're just a fool," the conductor said. "Just another goddamn fool. Why, some of you taxi drivers ought to be thrown off the street. The way you sonabitches drive—"

"Drop it, Mac."

"Drop what? I'm tellin' you what I think." He wanted violence with the taxi driver. The face of the driver was the face of each streetcar passenger who got on his nerves every day. "What I really ought to do is punch your head in."

"Try it."

"Oh, you want trouble? Sure, I'll give you trouble." The conductor swung clumsily and the driver rocked him with a hard right to the side of the head. The crowd backed away happily to give them all the room they needed. Then, as they lunged at each other, the crowd laughed and shouted and told them to go ahead and ruin each other.

In the rear of the taxi, Darby sat looking at the dark floor and smiling dimly as he remembered the creamy skin, the softness of Geraldine's shoulders. Like cushions of satin. And all the little details that added up to something really different. She painted her lips a glimmering orange, and used orange enamel on her fingernails. In restaurants she sat at the table sort of sideways, resting an elbow on the tabletop, her legs crossed and giving him side glances as she dipped her head to meet the food on the fork. She had a way of standing with her hands cupped just a few inches below her breasts, always that way, no matter what they were talking about. As though it wasn't too important, whatever they were talking about. But her breasts were sort of nice, weren't they?

Her breasts were really very nice. They came riding out in a kind of lazy way, always coming into view at just that moment, even if she'd been in the room for an hour. Not very big, but out there, firmly out there. And from

there on down the lines were slender and reservedly graceful, just hinting at something. Going down like that all
the way to the tips of her toenails, painted orange.

Well, that was six years ago. But come to think of it,
she'd been twenty-three then, and now, at twenty-nine,
the chances were she hadn't lost much of it. Maybe she
hadn't lost any of it. Maybe now it was there to an even
greater degree.

The electricity in the pale green eyes. And the moonlit-
water sheen of the platinum-blonde hair.

On the icy street the taxi driver took a roundhouse left
to the ear, flailed away at empty air, took another left to
the same ear, reached out and grabbed the conductor's
sleeve and pulled the conductor in close and kicked the
conductor in the shin. The conductor bent low and
butted the taxi driver in the stomach. The crowd
screamed with glee.

Darby shook his head slowly, disagreeing with what
Harry Clawson had said. Harry had said the personality
was pure poison, and that wasn't entirely correct. There'd
been times when her manner was high-grade honey, not
at all thick and sticky, not at all sugary. Just the right
flavor. So that the air around her was always filled with
pleasant little question marks, and an unheard sound,
like the faint tinkle of charming little bells that really
weren't there.

There were times when she talked far away from herself but it made sense anyway; when she expressed quiet
malice toward a world that needed, most assuredly, another flood. Toward all the greed and all the cheating.
All the masked filth. All the dirty rotten two-legged dogs
who didn't belong in the same street with the far cleaner
four-legged ones. Another flood, she insisted calmly, mostly for sanitary reasons. And she always qualified the statement, always backed up the argument with facts and figures when he protested that things weren't really that bad.

In the street, part of the crowd had to make way for
the taxi driver, who came sailing back from the force of
a sizzling punch in the nose. They let the driver fall
down. They let the conductor come in puffing and sob-

bing. The conductor slipped on the ice and went sideways and landed on a hipbone and couldn't get up.

In the rear of the taxi the darkness was gentle and velvety with pleasant memory, the little question marks and the little bells. The faint spicy fragrance, that special Japanese perfume she obtained somewhere. She told him it was made from oranges, to harmonize with the lips and the fingernails and the toenails. And sometimes she put an orange ribbon in the platinum-blonde hair.

The taxi driver opened the door and climbed in. He started the engine and put the taxi in reverse, took it off the streetcar tracks, and resumed the course going north on Kensington Avenue. He steered the taxi with one hand, and in his other he held a handkerchief, applying it sporadically to his mouth and his nose and his left ear.

Darby smiled placidly at the floor mat.

On the corner of Kensington and Allegheny he watched the receding taillight of the taxi, a little red eye that winked at him and said good-by as it went away down the snow-banked street.

He crossed Allegheny and walked along Kensington. As the street stretched away from the busy intersection the store fronts were smaller and gradually they became the shabby little shops struggling to keep alive. Some of them were already dead, and instead of merchandise in the windows there was only a curtain, to show it just didn't pay to stay in business, and now me and my husband we work in a factory.

He turned off Kensington and went past a tailor shop and a cigar store, past row houses pressed together as if there were a price on sunlight. At intervals a narrow alley showed itself. Some of the alleys weren't alleys at all, just a ribbon of space between the walls. Not wide enough for anyone to squeeze through, except the little kids, who found it useful when they played hide-and-seek. He passed one of these thin canyons and came to a stop, looking at the store window that showed only a curtain.

It was a sure bet she didn't live here any more. She must have left the neighborhood years ago. It was funny, the way he'd taken it for granted she'd still be here.

Someone had written a song about that. He couldn't
remember the name of it.

He stepped back a little, to get a wider view of the
store front. Memory floated around in little circles. All the
times he'd stood out here after they'd said good night and
the door had closed. Wondering why she wouldn't let
him kiss her. Wondering when he would really get to
know her. Wondering why he bothered at all.

And now it was as if she'd just said good night and the
door had closed. He sensed that although there was every
reason for concluding she'd moved away, she still lived
here. He stepped in toward the door and rang the bell.

He rang the bell several times. After all, there was
plenty of time. He wasn't headed any special place. Not
for a couple of hours, anyway.

He went on ringing the bell for more than a minute.
And then the door opened and he saw Geraldine.

The same Geraldine. The same pale green eyes. And
the platinum-blonde hair. She stood there in the doorway
wearing a cheap fur coat, with a lot of the fur eaten away.
She was wearing low-heeled slippers and one of her stockings had fallen down. But the orange lipstick was there,
and the orange-enameled fingernails. And the breasts
came into view even though the fur coat covered them.
She wasn't dressed to welcome a visitor, but that didn't
matter. It was just as Harry had said six years ago. The
looks were phenomenal.

For just part of a moment her eyes widened. Her lips
parted. But that was all. Immediately after that her face
was the same as it had been on all those nights when he'd
stood there at the door and she opened it for him.

And her voice was the same when she said, "I knew
you'd come back."

He smiled.

"Come on in," she said, and he followed her inside
through the same old rooms, down the narrow hall into
the same old parlor.

Nothing was changed, except that up in front it wasn't
a candy shop any more. Just an empty room with old
newspapers on the floor. But here in the parlor it was the

same as it had always been. The same rug. The same table.
And the couch.

"Take your coat off," she said.

"It's cold in here."

She pointed to a small electric burner. "That goddamn
thing is out of commission. I called the man three times."

"Maybe I can fix it."

"You think you can?"

"I'll try." He found, almost at once, that the trouble
was in the plug. The wire was loose. He started to work
on the wire, tightening the strands.

"Well," Geraldine said, "here he is," and laughed.

He was concentrating on the wire. "Got any adhesive
tape?"

"Sure." The little dry laugh again, trailing behind her
as she walked out of the room.

She came back and handed him the roll of tape. He
wrapped it around the tightened wire and secured the
wire in the plug. Then he inserted the plug in the socket.
The face of the burner began to glow orange.

She took off the fur coat. She was wearing a gray woolen
dress and he saw that one of the sleeves was patched. And
he realized, in the twisted moment, that there was a
change, after all. It had to do with the money she could
afford to spend on clothes. She had always been particular
about her clothes, even when there was very little money.
She had even admitted, at times, that she went without
lunches so she wouldn't have to buy cheaper shoes.

He wondered if there was any food in the house. But
she didn't look as though she was starving. And she
seemed perfectly content with the old furniture and the
shabby clothes.

"Sit down," she said. "Make yourself at home."

He got rid of the raglan and took a chair at the round
table in the center of the room. He offered her a cigarette,
but she shook her head. He lit one for himself. There was
no sound in the room.

Until he heard the purring voice. "Hello, Alvin."

On the couch, the green eyes glowed. And the hands
were cupped just a few inches below the breasts. With all

the little question marks floating around, and all the bells.

Something lifted him from the chair and took him across the room. He was on the couch with Geraldine. A filmy curtain began to come down on everything, and all the colors merged like the colors combining in a pool of oil. It seemed the couch was riding away from the platform of measured time, climbing toward some high place, way up high, where there were no hours or days or years.

The Japanese perfume was almost like a wave of sound. It hummed a dreamy little tune about a girl name Geraldine, who had eyes and ears and arms and legs, just like any other girl, but who certainly wasn't like any other girl. This little trick of unbuttoning his shirt—in the workaday world it was merely the process of freeing buttons from buttonholes, but the way Geraldine did it, it was a slow dance with the fingers, a weaving, floating dance of ten little sprites in magicland.

Her hand on his bare chest was satin and warm cream, but somehow cool within the warmth. She murmured something he couldn't hear, yet he knew the sound was there, the sound of a subdued cymbal, the signal that told him it was time to end the waiting and come back once again to the chamber of green fire, with the orange lips beckoning.

But all at once he heard another cymbal, far away yet louder, more urgent than the sound in this room. In that moment, as he felt the first light touch of the orange lips, he pulled away.

He got up off the couch and buttoned his shirt. He arranged his tie and straightened his jacket and put on the raglan. He moved toward the doorway and sensed the bluntness, the downright rudeness, of his abrupt leave-taking, but couldn't do anything about it.

Then he heard, as he walked down the hall toward the front door, the voice of Geraldine.

"Good night, Alvin."

Her knowing smile curled and coiled within her voice. Telling him it was only that, just good night. Making him know, ever so gently, that he could never really say good-by to Geraldine.

Chapter 11

ON THE WRIST-WATCH DIAL the hands read nine-ten. He was in a taxi riding downtown. Jutting above the front seat, the neck of the driver was a chunk of thick red beef under snow-white hair. The shoulders were wide and bulky, set there with a sort of obstinacy that went along with the mulelike progress of the taxi.

"Step on it," Darby said.

There was no sound from the front seat and the taxi wasn't going any faster.

"You hear me?" Darby said. "Let's get moving!"

Again the driver didn't reply, and it seemed now that he was purposely decreasing pressure on the accelerator.

"Hey, you." Darby leaned forward. "You got ears?"

"Easy, Jack." The driver had a voice like falling rocks rumbling. "Just take it easy."

"Easy, nothing. I'm in a hurry."

"Sorry, Jack. I can't help you. I'm driving with chains."

But still it seemed that the driver was doing it for spite. The taxi was crawling.

"Listen, you." And he wasn't at all aware of the icy hardness in his tone. "I told you to go faster. I won't tell you again."

Now the silence of the driver was a different kind of silence. It was on the order of worry.

But the shoulders were still obstinate, the taxi still crawled.

And the driver said, "All right, go ahead, report me to the company."

"Report you, hell. You know what's good for you, you'll hit that pedal."

The driver turned his head and saw the man sitting there in the back seat, the mussed-up straw-colored hair and the face completely expressionless. The coat collar was turned up and the man was slouched there with his hands in his coat pockets.

But then, a lot of them played tough when they weren't really tough at all. Some of them were nothing but damn fools who weren't happy unless they were putting on an act.

The driver decided that he had to find out. On these icy streets it was insane to go any faster, even with the chains. And his own natural toughness made the situation interesting for him.

"If you don't like it," he told the passenger, "I'll pull over to the curb. You'll get the hell out."

"Drive the taxi."

It was the tone. It told the driver he had better drive the taxi, and no kidding about it.

"And make it move. Beat that red light."

The driver found himself stepping harder on the accelerator and beating the red light.

"That's better," Darby said. "Keep it that way. Make time."

The driver half turned his head. "For God's sake—"

"Shut up."

"Now look, Jack—"

"I said shut up."

The bulky shoulders went up and down in a shrug. Why look for trouble? The taxi was doing thirty miles an hour. From the back seat the voice told him to go faster, and the taxi went up to thirty-five. Still faster, the voice said.

And the driver just had to say it. He couldn't help it. "What's wrong, Jack? You dodging the law?"

"No, I'm keeping an appointment."

"With what? A fire?"

"A man." His strategy fell away as the choked brain had to find an outlet. "A smooth lover boy. Real smooth. I want to see how smooth he is when he hits the floor."

"Gonna slug him?"

"Not slug. Slice."

The driver told himself he had acted wisely in making

the wheels go faster. There were no two ways about it. The voice in the back meant business.

The guy back there seemed rather willing to talk about it, so the driver said, "What'd he do?"

"Took my wife."

The driver smiled inside his lips. He felt a definite affection toward these fares that had wife trouble. It made this job of driving a hack seem almost worth while. Whenever they talked about it from the back seat, he let the taxi drive itself, his eyes still aimed through the windshield but somehow seeing the pleasant arena of other men's grief. It took him away, for a while, from the grief he had with his own wife, a fat woman he'd really enjoy strangling. Along with the little Filipino.

But his own thoughts in that direction were nothing more than vague wishes, and he felt a strange envy of the man in the back seat who wasn't going to let it pass, who was damn well going to do something about it.

"If you carve the bastard," he told his passenger, "get one in for me."

The chains clinked and clanked down Eighth Street. Past Spring Garden, past Buttonwood. They came to a stop at the corner of Eighth and Vine.

Darby got out and gave the driver a dollar tip.

He saw, some moments later, a middle-aged woman coming out of the door under the sign that read, "Pete's Cut-Rate Drugs."

He waited on the corner as the woman approached, and stood in the middle of the sidewalk to confront her. "Excuse me, madam—"

She gave a little cringe. "What is it?"

"That store you just came out of. How late is it open?"

He said it in a stiff, official sort of way that demanded a numerical answer and nothing else. City Hall was always making some kind of checkup in this neighborhood, and the woman told herself to tell the law what it wanted to know, and go on about her business.

She said, "Closes at eleven."

"Every night?"

She nodded emphatically. "Eleven sharp."

"All right," he said crisply. "Thank you."

He crossed the street and turned down Eighth. He looked at his watch and saw it was nine-fifty.

He looked up and saw, far down there below Race, the three golden balls swinging ever so lightly. A bright glow came from the window stocked with cheap jewelry and cameras and mandolins and brief cases.

He walked down Eighth and stood outside the pawn-shop. Three young men were inside, arguing with a short, bald man whose eyes were double size behind thick-lensed spectacles.

Finally they came to an agreement in there and the three young men walked out. Now, as they passed Darby, they were arguing among themselves. Two of them want-ed to go back to the crap game. The young man with all the money wanted to go on home.

Darby lit a cigarette. His surveillance of the merchan-dise in the window was critical, but sort of anxious, as though he really needed something special in there, but wasn't quite sure if it would make the grade.

The eyes inside the store made a slow, practiced ap-praisal of the raglan coat out there. Fine quality, the little bald man said to himself; he'd like to feel the fabric just to make sure. And then he noticed the sad disorder of the straw-colored hair, and reasoned that the wallet out there was more or less empty; the coat was just a souvenir from a time of better luck.

Now Darby had seen specifically what he wanted, and wondered whether its twin was in the store. His brain was geometric now, all the sharp angles of precisely ar-ranged strategy. He had to get it without buying it.

He entered the pawnshop.

The little bald man smiled a greeting. "Yes, sir?"

He wanted to look at the display cases. But not yet. For the time being, the talk would be strictly decoy. It would concern a saxophone. He reached back twelve and thirteen years to the days when he had played sax in the high-school band.

"I want a soprano saxophone. B flat."

The little bald man turned automatically to a row of

saxophones suspended on a rack behind the counter. "I got some dandies here."

"That silver one." Darby pointed. "Let me see it."

The man took the silver soprano off the rack and handed it to Darby. He waited tactfully as the saxophone was carefully examined. Darby tried all the keys, tried them again, and shook his head.

"The padding's no good."

"New padding wouldn't cost much. I'll give you a bargain."

"No," Darby said. "They charge too much for repairs. This won't do. Let's see that other one."

It was an aged gold-plated instrument, the plating worn off so the color was a dull dark yellow. He pressed the mother-of-pearl buttons and turned it around in his hands a few times and nodded approvingly.

"How much?"

"Almost nothing." The business mind was toying with figures. The ancient horn was practically unsalable and all it did was take up space. "I'll wrap it up for thirty dollars."

"Too high," Darby said.

"All right, I'll make you a present. Twenty-five."

"Fifteen."

The man laughed amiably. "It's a pity, you know? The Frenchman who made it would turn in his grave. When it was new it cost two hundred."

"It was new," Darby said, "before I was born."

The man took the saxophone from Darby and studied the length of it, a clumsy pretense of knowing something about saxophones. He looked up to see Darby smiling amusedly. He smiled in return, to tell the musician he wasn't really a sharper, he was only trying to make a living.

"Tell you what," he said. "Take it away for twenty."

Darby nodded. "That's good enough." He waited, knowing what was coming next.

The man said, "A case for it?"

"If you have any." Because there weren't any saxophone cases in view, and now everything depended on this, the fact that the saxophone cases would be somewhere in the rear of the store.

"I have some in the back," the man said, and in the same moment Darby was walking in behind the counter to make a casual study of the other saxophones. Timing the action on a split-second basis to watch the man going toward the rear of the store, to wait until the man entered a back room. After that it was rapid, and he pivoted to the display case containing the shiny-butted .22's and .38's, the penknives and switch blades and leather-sheathed hunting knives. He went toward the knife his eyes had caressed during the saxophone conversation, the pretty twin of the hunting knife on display in the front window. He had it in his hand and slipped it into the long, wide pocket of the raglan.

Now the knife was an accomplice that couldn't talk and couldn't work against him. Later, when the law asked questions, the pawnshop man could never say a knife had been purchased by a man with straw-colored hair, wearing a raglan coat. Ninety-nine times out of a hundred it was the weapon that gave the thing away. They had all sorts of methods of tracing the weapon. This was one weapon they'd never be able to trace.

He came out from behind the counter and moved slowly along, looking at catcher's mitts and fishing rods and glossy luggage of imitation leather. Suddenly he stopped and stiffened.

He knew, as if there were a mirror in front of his eyes, showing him what was in back, that he was being watched.

He turned and saw them there, outside the store.

Two of them. A tiny man with the face of a mouse, and a huge man wearing a ragged checkered cap and a sailor's pea jacket. With a mixed-up set of eyes and nose and lips somewhere between Dublin and Shanghai. Two uncanny creatures of the night, standing out there and grinning.

The panic existed for only a moment. After that it was strategy again, and the pattern remained geometric, not at all upset. He smiled back at the two who had seen him steal the hunting knife. As though to say, "Just wait out there, I'll be out in a minute. We'll make a deal and you'll forget what you saw."

As simple as that. Since that was all they wanted. Maybe a couple of bucks apiece, to go on their way and forget they'd ever seen him.

The little bald man came out from the back room, straining under the weight of several saxophone cases. He praised the quality of the leather, this one a genuine alligator, that one a genuine cowhide. Darby liked the one made out of cardboard.

"Eight dollars," the man said.

At most, Darby estimated, it was worth three. But add five for the hunting knife.

The man waited placidly for the bargaining to commence, telling himself he'd let it go for two and a half, and blinked behind the thick-lensed spectacles as he saw the wallet coming out. Twenty dollars for the horn, that's correct. Eight for the case. Thank you, sir. Shall I wrap it up?

Darby shook his head. He put the sax in the case, tucked the case under his arm, and walked out of the store, apparently ignoring the giant and the dwarf, who had to step aside to let him pass. But he waited for their footsteps to follow.

He took ten strides, stopped, and turned, edging sideways into the darkness of a flophouse doorway. They were walking slowly toward him, the big one with hands in the high pockets of the pea jacket, the little one using a fingernail for a toothpick.

They came toward him, while the bitter biting wind came in from the other direction. But he didn't feel the cold and he didn't mind the approach of strangers. He put a cigarette in his mouth and struck a match.

They arrived as though it were a scheduled meeting. The big one prodded his chin toward Darby's cigarette and said, "Got another?"

The little one took his finger away from his teeth. "I'll have one too."

He offered the pack, lit their cigarettes, and dragged gently at his own.

A pink glow came flowing down the stairway of the flophouse. It settled on the huge man, accenting the Chinese eyes and the Irish nose. But his mouth belonged to no special ancestry. His mouth was a sort of maw, never closed, with chipped and crooked rocks of teeth in the grayish gums. The thick lips flapping loosely as he said, "We seen you take it."

Darby nodded and waited.

The little one came inching in. The mousy eyes admired the raglan coat, traveled along the rich texture of the tweed to focus eventually on the saxophone case. "Pays for a horn and steals a knife. What about that?"

Darby didn't reply. He just went on waiting.

The huge man took off his cap and ran big fingers through pitch-black hair that hadn't been cut for months but was greased every morning and night. The fingers came down past stringy sideburns to caress the bristles on a red jaw. "Yeah," he mused aloud. "What about that?"

"It just don't figure," the little one said.

Darby blew smoke toward his shoes. "Does it need figuring?"

They both shook their heads, and the big one said, "All it needs is cash."

"Name it," Darby murmured.

The little one opened his mouth. "Let's say about—"

"Shut up, Rook," the huge man ordered, and Rook closed his mouth.

Then there was a lull, and Rook tugged at the big one's sleeve and said, "Come on, Chango. Wind it up. Can't stay here all night. Give him a price."

Chango's wide and cheery grin flowed toward Darby while he reached down idly with an immense paw that captured Rook's fingers and bent them backward. Rook's lips were stiff with pain.

"I told you to shut up." Chango's voice was softly thick, with a strange tenderness that told Rook they would always be chums, but Chango was boss. Then he released Rook's fingers and tossed the grin away and addressed Darby with market-place bluntness. "Fifty dollars."

Darby shook his head.

"Forty," Chango said.

"Can't be done," Darby murmured, and was curious to see what would happen if he turned away. He started to turn.

The big hand had his arm, very gently but with all the iron power firmly specified. Chango said, "You did larceny." He tightened the grip on the arm, as if he were the law speaking. "If you go up, you'll do six months."

Darby looked up at the eyes a head higher than his own. "Let go my arm or I'll knock your teeth out."

For only an instant Chango was amazed. After that he was delighted. He sent a grinning stare toward the mouse. "You hear that, Rook? He says he'll knock my teeth out. As if he really means it."

He let go of Darby's arm and stepped back with pleased wonder. He murmured admiringly, "Sure. He means it. A gamecock, sure enough. I bet he'd be a lot of fun."

But Darby went on past that. He had his wallet out. He extended a five-dollar bill. "Two and a half apiece. Take it or leave it."

Rook was contemptuous, though his eyes were on the money. "You're kidding."

"No," Chango decided. "He ain't kidding. I could tell if he was. He won't go a dime higher."

And took the five-dollar bill.

"That makes it a deal," Darby said.

But it seemed, as Chango pocketed the bill, that the deal was secondary. His eyes were on Rook as he aimed a thumb at the raglan coat. "I like this soldier. He knows what he's doing."

"You think so?" Rook's head was slanted while his eyes probed the expressionless face under the straw-colored hair. "I'll tell you what I think. I think this," and his forefinger described a little circle near his temple.

It was an angle Chango hadn't considered. Now, as he considered it, he found it interesting. "Could be," he mumbled. And then, as though Darby weren't there, "This is the street they come to. When they can't add the score on any other street."

Darby laughed without sound. He made a path for

himself between the two men and went on his way, north
on Eighth Street. They stood there staring at him. Rook's
forefinger did it once again, describing the little circle
near the temple.

The hanging sign read, "Pete's Cut-Rate Drugs."
He stood motionless on the other side of the street,
staring at the sign. Nothing was happening, but his eyes
were wide, and glittered as if something terrible was happening. Inside his head, a carefully built structure was
falling apart. It was the structure of strategy, and he could
feel all the measured segments dropping away from the
geometric plan. He felt the way he had when he was a
child and had built a house with playing cards, with
delicate manipulation, painstaking precision, only to see
the house give way and crumble, for no good reason at all.
Then he would get sore about it and throw the playing
cards all over the room.
He spotted a rubbish can near the curb and walked over
slowly and let the saxophone case fall in. He knew it was
a very stupid thing to do. He thought of all the other
places where he could have deposited the case containing
the B-flat soprano, all the strategic places, so much more
strategic than this rubbish can directly across the street
from the sign that read, "Pete's Cut-Rate Drugs."
He knew it was a bad mistake, but was unable to do
anything about it. He was unable to look at his wrist
watch, unable to design a single move. All he could do
was stand there, with a hand in his pocket, the fingers
curled around the knife.
The dial of the wrist watch said, to eyes that weren't
looking, ten-forty.
He stood on the curb, eight inches above the asphalt.
It became a diving board a hundred feet above the water.
He stepped off the edge, and felt the pull of empty
space taking him down.
As though the lit window were something way down
there underneath the deep black water. As though there
were no such thing as dimension or mathematical law or
any kind of law.

Chapter 12

A WOMAN WHO STOOD five feet four and weighed over three hundred pounds was buying a bottle of reducing pills. She gazed wistfully at the glistening black hair of Pete Lanson and his perfectly arranged features, all adding up to smooth good looks that blended with the silky-smooth voice as he told her how wonderful this stuff was. She pictured in her mind the magic scene of a few months from now, when she'd walk in and he'd take one look and immediately go on the make.

She bought the stuff, knowing it wouldn't work. Nothing worked; she'd tried just about everything. As she turned to leave the store, her mood became rebellious and she thought, to hell with it. Go on home and open the icebox and take out the rice pudding. And just then she saw the man who stood near the door, smiling at her.

It was an awfully pleasant smile. It said, You're nice, I like you.

But that couldn't be, she told herself. The man was much too good-looking to go for a fat slob who was the same width all the way down.

She sighed and walked out. Darby continued to smile at her. He felt quite friendly toward this woman who was making a tactful exit, leaving him alone in the place with Pete Lanson.

He heard the soft exclamation. "It can't be Al Darby!"

"Hello, Pete."

And he fully expected that Pete would react with whitened face and widened eyes. Even though Pete was such a smooth operator, such a calm bluffer, a stud-poker expert, it just wasn't possible for Pete to hide the dismay.

Yet Pete was doing it. He was coming out from behind the counter with the same old satiny smile, moving with that leisurely gait, as though this were nothing more than the greeting of an old friend he hadn't seen for a long time.

There it was, the sleek black hair, the jet eyes full of life and humor, the perfect nose above a thin mustache, the perfect lips that smiled blandly and seemed to say, Good old Al. I know why you're here, and what you have in mind. But it can't be done. I'll watch you like a hawk. I'll be ready for any move you make.

Pete wasn't dressed for selling cut-rate drugs. He wore a dark gray cardigan jacket and under that a long-collared pale gray gabardine sports shirt that required no tie. His slacks were gray hound's-tooth tweed, and his thick-soled sandals were the color of butter. He looked like some figure in a travel ad telling everybody to go to Miami and really live.

But then, long ago, when Pete had been selling refrigerators, he'd never dressed for that job, either. He'd always looked as though he were on vacation. Even on the hottest days of summer, when everyone was wilted and it was impossible to keep a crease in your pants, Pete was cool and keen like a long frosted drink, the white shirt spotless, the shantung trousers looking as if they'd just come off the press.

With all the girls flocking around, and all the light laughter that tried to hide their yearning for the unobtainable, the prize package that allowed itself to be tasted but never captured. The fascinating Lanson, the most popular lad in the crowd.

Pete was shaking his hand. Just the right pressure. The eyes were unblinking, with all the cunning underneath the pleasant smile.

Pete murmured, "How long has it been?"

"About four years." He told himself to take it slow, very slow, and found, in that line of thinking, a certain steadiness that adjusted his voice to just the correct pitch. "Thought I'd drop in and say hello. I happened to be in the neighborhood."

The smile stayed on Pete's lips, but his eyebrows went up a trifle. "What're you doing around here?"

He was ready for that. His own smile was on the slightly wicked side, a little touch of mischief. "I work hard, Pete. It gets monotonous. Every once in a while I like to play."

The eyebrows went up higher. "Around here? On Skid Row?"

He shrugged. "Anywhere I feel like playing. Depends on the mood I'm in."

"You?" The mild amazement contained a recollection of the quiet, conservative Al Darby, who never drank except for a beer or two, and never seemed quite comfortable when the parties got wild.

His reply held onto the mischief. "Why not?"

It was Pete's turn to shrug. "No special reason. As they say, all work and no play, et cetera. But somehow," and his gaze was thoughtful, going past Darby, "where you're concerned, it doesn't seem to fit."

"You'd be surprised, Pete."

For some moments Pete didn't answer. His thoughtful gaze continued to float past Darby. It was suddenly an important moment in the poker game, as though Pete's bluffing had been overshadowed by five better cards. Or a better bluff.

Finally Pete's eyes returned to Darby. And Pete said, "This business of getting around. Is this something new?"

"More or less."

But then, before it could go any farther, Pete shifted his position and leaned back against the display counter, his lean body graceful and relaxed.

The casual query drifted from Pete's lips: "How'd you come to locate me?"

He was like a boxer sliding inside a left hook. "Just happened to be passing by and I saw you in the window."

Then he moved backward just a little to get a better view of his target. His eyes, aiming at Pete Lanson, widened their focus to take in the length of the display counter going down toward the door in the rear. He wondered if the door led to an alley or whether there was another room in the back. He told himself to deal the cards very slowly and play it very close to the vest.

Because now it was major-league stud poker, it was higher mathematics. He was searching for a method to maneuver Pete down the length of the store and take him into that room, that alley, or whatever it was back there on the other side of the door.

And Pete's eyes seemed to say, No dice, Al, you can't fool me, I'm too smart for you.

Pete's voice said smoothly, "Tell me, how's Vivian?"

"Just fine."

"She's a high-quality girl," Pete said. "I envy you."

He just stood there, looking at Pete.

But Pete didn't see the look. Pete's eyes were on the floor. "I don't know, I guess it's reached the point where I'm fed up. This bachelor routine, it's strictly from nowhere. I'm just sick and tired of running around. Last week I flew to Chicago. And flew back the next day. For no good reason at all."

He wondered what he should say to that. He decided to say nothing.

"Every goddamn night," Pete said, "I close up at eleven and run out of here like an animal getting out of a cage. And then what?"

"Fun."

"Fun, hell. It just isn't fun any more. I can't seem to get any kind of a lift. Some nights I say to myself, What is it with you? What do you want?"

He found himself getting interested in what Pete was saying. As though Pete really meant it and it wasn't part of the bluff.

"I'm thirty-one years old," Pete went on, "and already I feel played out. This stomach trouble, the doc tells me it's mostly nerves. He says I'm all keyed up. About what? That's what I'd like to know."

After that it was quiet, and the moments swung back and forth like a pendulum, until Pete said, "It doesn't make sense. It's like a crazy steeplechase, and no finish line. I drink, I gamble, I hop from place to place like a jack rabbit. And money? You'd think I sat up nights, figuring ways to throw it away. Last year I cleared ten grand. I spent twelve."

Darby let his eyes rest on Pete Lanson's wrist watch. The band was navy-blue suede. The numerals were chips of sapphire.

Pete saw what Darby was looking at and raised his wrist, regarding the watch with a tempered disdain. "Four hundred and seventy-five dollars. And this is nothing. I got rings I never wear. Got a tie clasp with an emerald in it. And what for? Who am I trying to impress?"

Darby said nothing. He was trying to get back on the path of his own thinking. Yet it seemed that he was glued to the track of Pete's subjective comments.

"I'll tell you what's wrong with me," Pete went on. "I'm bored, that's all. I'm bored to tears. It's like a ferris wheel. Playing the horses. Watching floor shows. Getting to bed in broad daylight. And once you're on the wheel you can't get off, you just can't."

Darby told himself to be very careful. In every sense this Lanson was a salesman, and he knew every trick in the book. Especially when it came to lowering the customer's guard.

"I know what I need," Pete said, and his tone was urgent, almost grim. "I need a wife."

The pendulum swung back and forth, back and forth.

Pete nodded in emphatic agreement with his own statement. "A nice girl. Pure and sweet. Genuine." He looked straight at Darby. "Like your wife."

Darby heard a weird little sound. It was his own laughter, and as it trickled from his lips it had the taste of salt.

He told himself this Lanson was really brilliant. The bastard ought to go to California and win himself an Academy Award.

Pete said, "If I had a wife like Vivian, I wouldn't run out nights."

He laughed again. His words were just a thin veneer above the poison in the laughter. "You giving me a lecture?"

Pete shrugged. "Oh, what the hell. It's none of my business."

"Tell me what you think. I'd really like to know."

"You would? All right, then." The tone was kind and friendly. "I think you're a damn fool." He pointed toward the rear of the store, toward the stolid oblong of a phone booth. "Get in there, for God's sake, and call her up. Tell her you're coming home."

Darby laughed. "I can't do that. I have a date."

"Important?"

"More important than going home."

Then again the silence was the slow swing of the pendulum, and Pete gazed out past Darby's head, out past the plate glass of the front window, as though trying to see an answer out there.

Darby told himself the answer was right in here, in the left-hand pocket of his raglan.

He said, catering to a sudden hunch, "Where do you stay, Pete? In town?"

Pete continued to gaze out the front window. His tone was vague. "I live upstairs."

So the hunch was correct. That made it convenient. Now then, work it gradually, keep it delicate, and let's see if we can get him to take us upstairs.

The frown on Darby's face was incredulous. "Don't tell me you live in this neighborhood."

Pete used a different kind of frown. "Why not?"

"The atmosphere."

"You mean cheap?" And then Pete grinned. "Don't kid yourself. When you see my apartment you'll forget about the neighborhood. Come on up, I'll show you something."

They started through the store toward the door in the back. But suddenly Pete stopped. He looked up at the clock on the wall. It read three minutes past eleven. Pete turned and walked to the front of the store and locked the door. He pressed a button that put out all the lights except the green glow coming from the neon in the front window. He came back to stand behind Darby.

Inside himself, Darby smiled. He said, without sound, That's right, Pete. Keep in back of me. So you can watch every move I make. But you see, I'm in no hurry. I'll wait it out. You're bound to slip.

Pete stayed behind him as they arrived at the back door. He opened it, revealing a storage space and a window that loooked out on an alley. He told himself the alley would be convenient as he turned to the stairway on the right.

The stairway went no higher than the second floor. And that was another convenience to keep in mind, the fact that Pete Lanson was the only tenant in this building.

Pete's apartment was really something to see. The rooms were large, the furniture was sleek and costly. Pete said he paid a girl twenty dollars a week to keep the place scrubbed and dusted.

They came into the bedroom, high-ceilinged and carpeted in dark green broadloom, with dark green walls and an immense rectangular oil painting of some women taking a bath in a river.

He was looking at the painting.

Pete stood behind him.

Darby said, "I like this. I think it's great."

"Cost me plenty."

"Look at what he put there." He pointed toward a clump of trees on the other side of the river.

"Where?" Pete asked.

"There." He moved his finger so Pete couldn't see specifically what he was pointing at.

Pete remained behind him. "I don't see anything special. What is it?"

"A giraffe."

"A what?" Pete asked.

"Giraffe," he said. "See the long neck? Right there, behind the trees."

Pete stepped in front of him, went in close to the painting, Pete's nose almost touching the canvas as he searched for the giraffe that wasn't there.

"Keep looking," Darby said. "You'll see it."

Pete laughed and said he couldn't see it and maybe he needed glasses. Or maybe Darby needed glasses. It became a little game of find-the-giraffe and Pete went on with his scrutiny of the painting.

Darby stood directly behind Pete. He moved his fingers

toward the left-hand pocket of the raglan. His fingers went in and felt the leather of the sheath containing the hunting knife.

Pete was saying something but he didn't hear Pete's voice. He heard, instead, a voice from very long ago.

A voice that said, Don't, don't, don't.

It was the voice of his sister Marjorie. She came running toward him across the dark green grass of Fairmount Park, and he stood there, twelve years old, with a rock in his hand, taking careful, hateful aim at the other boy, who retreated slowly through the moonlight.

"Don't," Marjorie cried. "Please don't."

"Get out of the way," he told Marjorie. "I'll knock his brains out. I'll kill him."

Marjorie stood with her arms spread wide, an obstacle in his path of attack. "Alvin," she pleaded, "put that rock down. What's the matter, you crazy or something?"

"I'm gonna kill him, that's what I'm gonna do," and he tried to aim past Marjorie, his lips trembling, his eyes wild as he stared at the other boy, so much taller and older than himself, old enough to smoke cigarettes and drive a car and take girls for walks in Fairmount Park.

Marjorie changed her tone from plea to stern command. "Now listen, young man. You behave yourself." She came closer and made a move to take the rock.

He backed away. Sharp pains were shooting through his chest. He blinked hard, telling himself he mustn't cry. "What are you doing, taking up for him?" He tried to gulp down the weight in his throat. "I saw what he was doing. Right there, in them bushes—"

"Alvin—"

"And you too, you weren't even trying to stop him." His voice burned with jealousy, and his utter misery and disappointment made his knees weak. "I saw you," he choked. "I saw you kissing him."

"But Alvin," and her voice was soft again, "there's nothing wrong in kissing him. He's my boy friend."

"No!" He wanted to scream it. But it was only a sob. And then, gasping, "He isn't, he isn't, he can't be your boy friend. I'm your boy friend."

"But it's different with you. Can't you see? You're my brother."

And then, forgetting the rock in his hand, and the target retreating back there among the trees, and his eyes stabbing accusingly at Marjorie, "You told me I was your boy friend. You said it that day in the kitchen. You said I was your best boy friend."

Marjorie moved toward him, seemed to float toward him. Her face was softly radiant in the moonlight. Her pale green eyes were suddenly lit with a strange fire. "You are," she said. And then, as though he weren't there for a moment, as though she were all alone, "Oh, no. It's only my kid brother. Only twelve years old." But somehow she was not able to stay with the moment. She came closer to him, and closer.

"Hold me," she said. "Put your arms around me."

His arms reached out. The green fire blazed from her eyes and into his eyes and then they were walking together across the dark green grass and headed toward the bushes. And the sky was like a dark ceiling that went sliding down to bring the moon nearer, while the spring-time grass became a pillow that caressed his cheek and the fragrance of violets was all around. And all around. He heard the moaning and the sighing and the sound of the squirming because they were hugging and kissing in the bushes and then there was no sound at all for some time but suddenly there was a smothered cry and he heard Marjorie saying, "Don't, don't, don't."

She cried out again, louder, and he wondered what he had done.

He could feel the hunting knife in his hand. Directly in front of his eyes the cardigan jacket was an easy target. But he couldn't move his arm and he was telling Marjorie to go away.

And he heard Marjorie saying, No.

He told Marjorie to keep out of this, it didn't concern her.

She said, You're wrong, it does concern me. Just wait and let me tell you, please let me explain.

He shoved Marjorie aside. And then his arm was free. His arm moved. It took him forward and down and into a dark chamber where he stared at the thing on the floor.

He ran out of the bedroom, ran down the stairs, and opened the door that led to the alley. In the alley the snow had hardened and it looked like glass with milk underneath. He raced down the alley and slipped and fell.

He heard, just then, a voice that was real. It was the voice of Pete Lanson.

Pete was shouting, "Al, what's wrong? Come on back."

Across the milky ribbon of the alley he saw Pete walking toward him.

He got up and ran.

"Al, come back. Hey, for God's sake—"

He ran as fast as he could, with Pete's voice fading behind him. Everything was fading.

Except what his fingers could actually feel. He had them in the left-hand pocket of the raglan. He took out the hunting knife, still in its sheath, where it had been all along. He looked at it and smiled at it and hurled it over his shoulder, hearing the soft thud as it hit the snow.

Presently he stopped running. He just moved along in a sort of shamble.

He came out on Eighth Street and joined the shambling parade of blank-faced men who had no place to go.

Chapter 13

Bluish light came from a plate-glass window and fell on the shivering colored man who stood outside looking in. The colored man was in his late thirties and had an unlit calabash pipe in his teeth. He was tall and very thin and wore a tattered camel's-hair cap with ear flaps and a knee-length mackinaw blocked in bright green and black and yellow. His corduroy trousers were olive green, tucked into the unhooked tops of his galoshes.

Darby wondered what the man was looking at, and walked up to the plate-glass window and saw it was a Chinese shirt laundry. In there at the shirt presses the Chinese girls and colored girls were working with a kind of frantic speed, oblivious of the rule of slow traffic out here on Eighth Street. Two Chinese men, obviously the owners of the establishment, were walking up and down past the shirt presses, their hands behind their backs, their eyes on the floor.

"All night long," the colored man said.

Darby looked at the calabash pipe. "Why don't you smoke it?"

"Got no tobacco."

"Buy some." Suddenly it was very important that the colored man should smoke the calabash pipe. It was more important than anything else.

The colored man silently agreed. He took the big-bowled pipe from his mouth and gazed at it regretfully. "Ain't got one penny."

"I'll get you some," Darby said. He hurried up the street and went into a store and bought a packet of pipe tobacco. He came back and handed it to the colored man.

The colored man filled the calabash and lit it expertly. The thick blue smoke drifted from his lips and became part of the bluish glow flowing from the laundry window.

"Look at them," the colored man said, his eyes on three tiny Chinese girls whose arms were flexible blades, hacking away at the shirts. "Look at them go."

Darby watched the whirring action, the shirts lifted from a basket, placed on the presses, the presses slamming down, and the neatly folded shirts arriving on the neat pile.

He estimated there were a few thousand shirts on the wide tables, and said, "They do a nice business."

"You know it too?"

"Shirts get dirty," he said, as though he had just discovered the fact. "A man likes to wear a clean shirt."

"True, man. Quite true."

"Wash the shirts. Iron the shirts. Make money."

"Talk, man. Talk more like that."

"Work all night. Stay inside. Out of the cold."

"And then go home," the colored man said. "Tell me about that."

Darby nodded. "Home. All tired out. Look at the bed and get the good feeling. Go to sleep."

"No, not yet," the colored man said. "Stay with the good feeling. Let me hear about that."

"Hot in the room. The radiator makes a noise. Zing, zing, the steam. Outside, the wind, the snow. Cold out there. But in here in the room, nice and hot. With the lights out. And the husband there—"

"Now let me take it," the colored man said, with his eyes going through the plate-glass window and gently patting the soft arm of a little brown-skinned girl who was marking shirts. "The husband there in the bed in the room with the lights out. Well, girl, put the lamp on. The little lamp with the orange bulb. You, Woodrow. Hey, Woodrow, wake up, man. Sit up. Look at her. Here she is. Come home from work. To you. Next room, all the kids. Five, six, seven kids. Think of that. Yours and hers. Woodrow and Clotile."

"Your name Woodrow?"

The colored man nodded.

"I'm Alvin."

"Hello, Alvin." He pointed to the brown-skinned girl who was marking shirts. "That's Clotile. We busted up a year ago. Tell you how. I write music, see? Not jazz. Real music. From the heart, you know? But she, Clotile, she don't appreciate that. Says, 'Go on, man, go on out and get a job.' Says, 'I'm tired working all night in the Chinese laundry and you sit home all day and scribble that mess and can't sell one song.' I say to myself, She's right, you know? Makes me ashamed. I go out and get a job. On the docks. Late shift. Come home one night and find her in the bed with a man."

Darby watched Clotile as she placed some shirts on wrapping paper and folded the paper over the shirts. In the midst of doing it, she paused and wearily drew her forearm across her brow. Then she leaned over to look at another girl's wrist watch. She sighed deeply and went on working.

He started to feel sorry for her, but was pulled back by the voice of Woodrow.

Woodrow was saying, "She and him, right there in the bed. Well, I just stand there, you know? And he, you know what he does? Sits up and talks big. You see, he's been here before. Now it's his house. Says somebody's got to go, and it ain't gonna be him. Well, me, I just play it cool. Say, Good night, all, and go out. Out, hell. Out to the kitchen, what I mean. Get me an ice pick. Come back and put it on him. Yow, the man yells. And out he goes, out the window. I say to Clotile, 'Tell the man to come back tomorrow night,' and she says, 'You mean that?' And I say, 'Girl, you know I mean it.' I put my clothes together in a bag. I say 'Good-by, Clotile.' And I cut out."

"And never went back?"

"Never," Woodrow said. "But some nights it's so cold, like tonight. Seems there ain't no way to get warm. I come here and just stand and look in the window. At Clotile. And you know what? It warms me. That's Clotile in there, that's my woman."

"Why don't you go back?"

"Back? To that no-good tramp?"

"Come on," Darby said. "Let's go."

Woodrow took the calabash from his mouth. "Go where?"

"Anywhere."

Woodrow's eyes were dubious. "You say your name is Alvin, but I don't know who you are. You look all right, you sound all right, but I don't know."

Woodrow took a backward step.

"No," Darby said. "Don't go away."

It was the timid pleading of someone afraid to be alone in the woods. Woodrow frowned at the pavement and said aloud to himself, "What's he puttin' down?" Then he looked up to study Darby's eyes. "If you're one of them sissies you don't want me." Then he shook his head emphatically. "But you can't be that. I know you ain't that."

Darby stared past the green-black-yellow mackinaw. "Just don't go away."

Woodrow moved in for a closer appraisal of the eyes. He declared solemnly, "You're high. You're way up. And not on whisky, either."

The vague grin and the blinking. "Way up where?"

"In the clouds." He went on studying the eyes as though reading a meter. "Up ten thousand feet. But that ain't enough, is it, Alvin? You want to go higher. Up there past the moon."

It sounded like a pleasant trip, and Darby nodded.

"On a new kind of rocket," Woodrow said. "Goes up slow. Nice and lazy, slow circles. Going up."

"The rocket?"

Woodrow took the calabash from his mouth and held it tenderly, as if he were holding the stem of a flower. "There's always room for one more passenger."

They walked together down Eighth Street.

Where the winos and hopheads gathered, the tender-loin had its own United Nations. They came here, the Chinese and the Africans, the Swedes and Peruvians and

Scots, the Frenchmen and the Australians. They came and
went and came back again to the dimly lit room that had
no furniture, only the bottles on the floor, the cans of
snuff, the little paper boxes containing the condensed
kick of a thousand mules.

Bring your own supply. Or bring the money to buy
some of mine. If you smile at me right, you'll get it for
free. You want muscatel? It's here. You want the white
stuff, the cooked corn? You want the real cheap wine,
the Sneaky Pete? It's all here, in the Hall of Joy. Almost
anything you crave, except the more expensive merchandise that we'd like to have but we can't afford it.

We have pitchers of beer that becomes more than beer
when you add a couple of cigarette ashes. And the snuff,
we have a cute little caper with that, we blend it with
aspirin tablets and then put in any kind of cola drink
and the total is the feeling you get just before the roller
coaster starts the downward lunge. But you don't come
down while you're in this room. Here it's the place of the
take-off, the climb to the next higher level, and taking
off again. Always going up.

With the shiny little blue tablets, mostly caffein. With
the gray powders and the white powders that you sniff
with your eyes half closed. With paper bags that you put
over your head so you won't waste any smoke from the
sticks of marijuana. Then you slowly lift the bag and
see the violet moon, so close you can touch it.

But don't touch it. You'll burn your fingers. It's the
flame of the big candle on the mantelpiece. With the
smaller candles on the floor and on the window sills. You
see, there's no electricity here. And no plumbing. The
city condemned this place a long time back, and they're
always planning to tear it down. But somehow it stays
up. One day they'll go ahead and put the wreckers to
work. But that won't matter much. The winos and hopheads will find another place. They always manage to
find a place.

Now, while they have this haven, they come here to
the big room on the second floor, with the windows
boarded to hide the candlelight from the prowl cars on

the street. Not that they fear the law; they've been picked up so many times it's become a routine thing. It's just that the law is an interruption, an irritation. When you're up here in cloudland, you want no interference.

He stood there in the doorway with Woodrow and saw the faces in the candlelight. The faces were of many races, but they seemed to be all one color, a violet-gray-yellow against the colorless mass of decaying walls. Some of them were just standing still with nothing to lean against, some were leaning against the walls. Some sat on the window sills, on the floor, and some were flat on the floor. Others appeared to be neither on the floor nor anyplace else, just floating in the smoky glow.

The noise in the room was a mosaic containing the drone of a man talking to himself, another man talking to the entire world, a little group of winos singing a calypso, a colored woman telling a Portuguese man that she was seventy-eight years old, while the Portuguese sullenly insisted she wasn't a day over forty. And far over there, in a corner all by himself, a boy from the hills of Tennessee crooned to a girl who was buried in the hills.

A fat Italian woman came walking across the floor toward Woodrow and Darby. She was very short and the fatness was loose, flapping and waddling, as though her clothes were filled with gelatine. Yet she moved with a definite vigor and her manner was that of an efficient supervisor as she addressed Woodrow.

"Who is this you bring?"

"The man's a friend of mine," Woodrow told her. He made the introduction. Her name was Anna.

She looked Darby up and down, and formed a swift conclusion. "A square."

Some faces were moving in to have a look at the newcomer. They moved in close and stayed there, as though to tell Darby they weren't yet ready to invite him in.

Anna put her hands on her hips, turned her face to the side, and looked at Darby from the corners of her eyes. "You got money?"

He reached for his wallet. All the faces leaned in.

Woodrow grabbed his wrist before his fingers could touch the pin seal.

"That ain't required," Woodrow told him. "Don't never show the finances. We got thieves in this office."

"You worried about it?" Anna asked Woodrow.

"Not when I'm the banker," Woodrow replied pleasantly, and directed Darby to hand him the wallet.

Darby gave it to him, and someone let out a brittle laugh. "Safe deposit."

"He'll get it back," Woodrow said evenly, and aimed a level gaze at the face that had laughed.

The face was the color of cordovan. The man was a Haitian, tall and stout and solidly packed. He wasn't laughing now, and he said to Woodrow, "Who you lookin' at?"

"At you," Woodrow said. He was lowering the wallet into a pocket of the mackinaw.

"Give it back," the Haitian ordered.

"So you can lift it?"

Anna stepped in between the Haitian and Woodrow. The Haitian caught Anna under the armpits, tried to push her aside, and discovered she was too heavy.

Someone told Anna to get out of the way and let them slaughter each other.

Then someone told everybody to watch out. In that instant the Haitian had a switch blade in his hand. He pressed the button and the mother-of-pearl handle sent the blade flicking out six inches.

In the same instant Woodrow reached out and obtained a half-filled bottle of corn. He held it by the neck, swinging it lightly as he calmly drew smoke from the calabash.

But just then a tiny black-skinned girl came running across the room, threw her eighty-seven pounds at the back of the Haitian, swung a fist that caught him just under the ear. As he turned, she hit him again, catching him in the eye. Then she punched him a third time, cutting his lip.

"Irma!" the Haitian cried. "Irma, what you doin' to me?"

The tiny girl kicked him in the shin. "What'd I tell you, Henry?" She kicked him again. "What'd I tell you 'bout pullin' that blade?" She grabbed at his hair and missed, and used her fist again, banging him on the forehead.

"Don't, girl," the Haitian whimpered. He had dropped the knife and now he cringed against the wall, lifting his arms to shield his face.

"Put your hands down, Henry," the girl commanded. She stepped back and took aim with her foot. She got him just under the knee. He let out a moan.

"Enough," Anna suggested.

Irma was breathing hard. "Enough? That blade of his, it's put him in jail three times. I got to teach him, Anna. I'm his woman. If I don't teach him, who will?"

She banged her fist against the eye she'd hit before.

Henry sat down on the floor. Irma stood there looking at him. After a few moments she sat down beside him and used the edge of her sleeve to wipe the blood away from his face. Someone handed her the mother-of-pearl switch blade and she took it and hurled it across the room, announcing, "Whoever picks it up can keep it."

Then Henry murmured something, and Irma uncapped a bottle of homemade dandelion wine. She held it to his lips, as if she were feeding a baby, and smiled the dim and faraway smile of knowing he belonged to her.

Gradually the sounds in the room were lower, the faces were quiet, and the eyes focused only on the bottles, the powders, the pills, and the sticks. Woodrow asked Darby what he'd like to drink, and Darby said he wasn't a drinker, so really it didn't matter, anything would do. Woodrow bought a bottle of muscatel from Anna.

Darby drank some muscatel and said he didn't like it. It was too sweet. Woodrow asked him what else he wanted, and he said he didn't know. Woodrow shrugged and busied himself with the muscatel.

They were seated on the floor, and their immediate neighbors were the Portuguese and the colored woman who had claimed she was seventy-eight years old. The

Portuguese continued to insist that he knew how old
she was, and he'd bet anything he had that she wasn't
past her fortieth birthday.

The colored woman didn't take it as a compliment.
She told the Portuguese he'd better go and have his eyes
repaired. She mumbled it absently while removing the
cap from a can of snuff.

She held the can over a porcelain bowl and shook
some snuff into the bowl, carefully measuring the
amount. The Portuguese solemnly handed her a small
tin box, and she opened it and took out several white
pills and dropped them into the bowl, one by one.

Darby was interested. He inched across the floor, lifted
his chin questioningly.

The woman extended her palm to display the white
pills. "This is aspirin," she told Darby. "We mix it with
the snuff."

"And then," the Portuguese said, "we put in some of
this." And he showed Darby the large-sized bottle of
carbonated water, cola flavored.

"Taste good?" Darby asked.

The Portuguese pointed to his mouth. "Not in here."
Then he pointed to his head. "In here, just fine. Delicious."

The woman was pouring cola into the bowl. Then
she had a spoon in her hand and she was stirring the
mixture of snuff and aspirin and cola. Darby leaned in
closer and looked in the bowl and saw the frothy, co-
coa-brown liquid that slowly swirled and seemed to smile
at him. Seemed to beckon.

Then the Portuguese lifted himself from the floor and
went away, and some moments later he came back, his
fingers ringed with the handles of three tin cups. He dis-
tributed the cups to the woman and Darby and himself.

The woman dipped her cup into the bowl with a
practiced flicking motion that got the cup exactly half
full. The Portuguese did the same.

"Now you," the woman said to Darby.

The cup was steady in his hand. He lowered the cup
into the bowl, doing it slowly, with a kind of ceremonious

grace, as though he fully appreciated the dignity attached to this initiation. He lifted the half-filled cup and held it poised, waiting politely while the older members took the first sip.

They lowered the cups from their lips and nodded to him. The woman said, "Just a little, now. Just a little at a time. You drink it too fast and you'll ruin the insides."

He tasted the mixture. The perfect blending had erased the individual flavor of snuff and aspirin and cola, to make the total a strange taste that couldn't be classified. He sipped the stuff and went on sipping it, and some minutes later he began to hear the liquid melody of a newly invented stringed instrument. The strings were made of velvet.

The cups were dipped again in the bowl.

The floor became soft, then softer, then had no pressure at all, just the gentle cushion of lots and lots of flower petals.

And the walls went sliding up, and the ceiling went up. Everything was going up.

So nicely. So easily. Just floating up past the roof.

Then going up and up in the slow, lazy circles. It felt so good, it was a wonderful way to travel. More comfortable, more safe than any other way.

He was going up in a fine, spacious vehicle that couldn't stall, couldn't break down, and always had room for one more passenger.

The marvelous rocket never lurched, never wavered, and made no noise except for the velvet melody, and the pleasant purring noise coming from the circle of faces in the glow of candlelight. It turned slowly, mixing the ceiling with the floor; mixing the four walls and making it one wall; and mixing the faces until gradually it was only a few faces and finally it was one face.

The adorable face with the sweet and tender smile.

The face of his sister Marjorie.

"But you can't be here," he murmured. "You went away long ago."

A hand touched his arm. He turned and saw the Portuguese. He heard the logical question, "Who went away?"

"Marjorie."

"Who is Marjorie?"

"My sister."

"She pretty?"

"Yes," he said. "She was really very pretty."

The colored woman leaned over and lightly tapped her finger against the chin of the Portuguese. She said, "You do that all the time. You mustn't do it."

"Do what?" the Portuguese asked.

"Get ideas," the woman told him. "A man's mother, a man's sister. It ain't right."

The Portuguese shrugged. "All I do is think about it."

"It ain't even right when you think about it." The woman turned to Darby. "Don't you worry. I won't permit it. Won't let no man get thoughts about your sister."

"I see her," Darby said. "She's here. I see her."

The woman nodded. "I can tell. You're lookin' right at her."

"Why?" He addressed the question to the sky. "Why do I always see Marjorie?"

The woman drew up her knees and put her arms around them and gazed past her folded fingers. "She older than you?"

"Three years older."

The woman considered this for a moment. Then her head went back very slowly, went all the way back as though she were trying to see the floor behind her. "Tell me, man. You got a wife?"

"No," Darby said.

"You got a woman?"

"No."

The Portuguese squirmed impatiently. "Tell me, mister. Tell me more about Margie."

"Now look, you." The colored woman jutted her lower lip toward the Portuguese. "I warned you about that."

The Portuguese ignored the colored woman. He moved closer to Darby and said, "Tell me about the looks. I like to hear about the looks. Is Margie built tall?"

"No," Darby said. "Just medium."

"That's good," the Portuguese declared. "I don't like them when they're tall. But tell me," and his eyes were bright with searching, "she weigh a lot?"

"No. Very slender."

That worried the Portuguese. "Like a broomstick?"

Darby shook his head. "No, not like a broomstick. Just very slender. Very pretty."

The colored woman wagged her finger with disapproval. "It ain't right," she muttered. "It just ain't right."

But the Portuguese had a feeling he was halfway there already, and he wouldn't be content until he was all the way there. He touched the heel of his palm against Darby's shoulder. "Tell me now. What color eyes?"

"Green."

"Like the grass?"

"No," Darby said. "Pale green."

"Oh," the Portuguese breathed. "I like that. I like that very much." He clapped his hands gently, making a soft and scarcely audible sound. "Now, the hair. What color hair?"

Darby didn't reply.

"The hair," the Portuguese said. "Tell me what color."

Darby rested back on his elbows. He distinctly heard the voice that wanted to know the color of Marjorie's hair. He wondered why he wasn't able to answer.

He saw the Portuguese and the colored woman looking at each other, then looking at him. He couldn't understand why they were frowning, as though they were stumped by some kind of puzzle.

He saw the Portuguese moving in again, felt the insistant pressure against his shoulder as the Portuguese demanded to know the color of Margie's hair.

"I can't remember," Darby said, but suddenly he did remember. He saw Marjorie facing a mirror, with a comb and a brush. And he murmured, "Dark hair. Dark brown."

The Portuguese continued to frown. "You sure?"

He nodded. He saw the Portuguese losing the frown and wondered why the colored woman was still frowning. He had the acute feeling that his answer wasn't sat-

isfactory to the colored woman. The feeling drilled farther into his brain, went deeper and deeper until it was
the actual pain of tissue getting torn from drilling. He
felt the warm wetness on his face, pouring down and
dripping onto his lips and tasting salty. He felt the quivering and tried to stop it and couldn't.

But then, as Marjorie smiled at herself in the mirror,
the comb and brush disappeared and were replaced by
something else. It was a bottle. A bottle of peroxide.

Chapter 14

Everything was hazy. Much too hazy for talk or any kind of motion or any effort at all. It was the passive drifting in the middle of the ocean, and no way to battle the tide, so why try? Without seeing anything special, the eyes took in the porcelain bowl and the empty bottle, the face of the colored woman and the sprawled legs of the Portuguese. He took in the smile of Irma as she leaned against the shoulder of her Haitian, and saw the calabash pipe dangling from the lips of Woodrow, who bowed formally from the waist as he presented Anna with a dollar bill and received more muscatel and fifty cents change. Then he saw it all going away and didn't know that he was headed toward the door.

At the door, Woodrow stopped him and asked him where he was going. He told Woodrow to leave him alone, he just felt like going. Woodrow looked hurt, and he told himself it wasn't the way to say good-by to a friend. He told Woodrow he was sorry, and he really didn't mean the impoliteness, he was just tired, that was all, and now he ought to go home.

Woodrow gave him the wallet. He took out a five-dollar bill, but Woodrow said no, and became indignant. Absolutely not, Woodrow said, and declared it would be outrageous to accept so much as a dime from someone who was twenty thousand feet up in the air. He had no idea what Woodrow meant by that. He knew only that Woodrow would need some money to buy more wine, and he wanted Woodrow to be happy with the wine. He insisted, and said he wouldn't leave until Woodrow accepted the five dollars.

So finally Woodrow accepted it, and guided him down the hall and down the stairs and out upon the street.

They said good night, and Woodrow went back inside.

Darby crossed the street and arrived at a hill of snow that appeared too high for climbing. He walked along the base of it, looking for an opening so he could get through and reach the sidewalk. Headlights flashed in his eyes, and the horn honked frantically. He threw himself sideways, hitting the snow as the car whizzed past. He wondered if he should spend the night here. Perhaps the next car wouldn't miss.

He looked at his wrist watch and saw it was two-fifteen. He felt the icy pressure of the hard-packed snow against his face, and got up and went on walking, telling himself it might be a good idea to find a place to sleep.

He rounded a corner, went down Ninth, and followed Vine to Eighth Street. He started down Eighth and saw the sign above the flophouse doorway. It said the price was thirty-five cents. Without any further stipulations it said quite bluntly that you pay the thirty-five before you look at your bed.

There was nothing but the doorway and the stairway. He went up the stairs and saw an old man sitting at a table and reading a Greek newspaper. The old man asked him what he wanted and he said he wanted sleep. That was sufficient for the old man, who took the dollar bill and gave him his change and thumbed him toward the door behind the table.

Darby opened the door and saw the big room and the shaded electric bulbs hanging from the ceiling. All the bulbs were lit and some of the sleepers had handkerchiefs on their faces to protect their eyes from the glare. There were five rows of cots, eight cots to a row, and nearly all the cots were taken. Most of the men were asleep or trying to fall asleep, but some of the men sat on the edges of the cots and stared at the floor. Others stood in a silent group at the window facing Eighth Street. There was another group at the far end of the room, playing penny-ante poker and making their bets between grunts and coughs.

The sound of the room was mostly coughing. All kinds of coughs. The whisky cough, flat and dry. The wheezing tobacco cough, and the raw cough of a sore throat, the blood-filled cough of bad lungs, the wet and blobbery cough of a ruined respiration. Here and there the coughs were sliced with an occasional curse, a pronouncement of malice toward everything and anything.

Roaches ran in and out between the boards showing through the cracked plaster of the ceiling. The floor had its own unique carpet, softer than sand, and fully an inch thick: genuine dust. The soft, warm home for a thousand families of vermin. Other vermin liked the better climate up above, and made their homes in the mattresses.

The aisles between the cots were very narrow, and he had trouble moving up along the aisle where legs and arms and heads were flung out in all sorts of positions. He bumped into someone's leg and the man called him an unpretty name. Someone else told the man to shut up, and the man told the entire room to do something that was biologically impossible.

Toward the center of the room, Darby found an empty cot that seemed less filthy than the others. He sat down on the edge of it and took off his shoes. He started to take off the raglan and discovered, in that moment, that it was very cold in here. He buttoned the raglan and lifted his legs onto the cot. He arranged himself flat on his back, his arms crossed on his chest. The electric light came flooding through his closed eyelids, but he didn't mind. He was really quite comfortable, and now it would be nice to go to sleep.

The rude interruption was a hand taking hold of his foot and twisting his ankle. He opened his eyes and saw them: the Irish-Chinese giant, Chango, and the little one, the mouse, Rook.

Chango let go of Darby's foot and showed the wide wet grin. "You remember us?"

He nodded. Aside from that, he didn't move.

"We followed you," Chango said.

He wasn't irritated. He wasn't bothered at all. In a moment of crystal-clear objectivity he sidestepped away from himself and took a look and knew that he had passed the point where anything could bother him. Then the moment passed and he came back to himself, the quiet and pleasant companion who cruised along so easily.

Rook went around to the other side of the cot and sat down on the edge of it, as if he were visting a patient in a hospital. "How d'you feel?"

"Fine." He sat up slowly, showing a mildly puzzled smile. "You followed me all the way?"

"Not all the way," Rook replied. "Saw you go in the store. Lanson's place. Saw you in there, chatting with Lanson. Then he puts out the light. We didn't see you come out. So we lose you. Until a few minutes ago we see you coming in here."

He was very tired. Vaguely he wished they'd go away so he could get some sleep. But somehow it wasn't at all difficult to sit up. He didn't know that Chango's arm was providing the backrest.

He heard Chango saying, "Here, take this," and felt the cigarette inserted between his lips. He saw the flaming match and pulled at the cigarette, pulled too much smoke and choked on it and coughed.

"Easy does it," Rook said.

He wondered what that meant. And who had said it. He blinked several times, but it didn't help his eyes. For some unaccountable reason his eyes were out of commission and everything was blurred.

He tried to lower himself to the mattress, but it was as if he were sitting in a chair. The back of the chair was made of iron and wouldn't give an inch.

He heard a low, rumbling voice say, "You know Lanson?"

His head was moving from side to side. He put forth an effort and managed to nod.

"You friendly with Lanson?"

He looked at Chango and said, "No. Not friendly. Not at all."

"Why'd you go in there?"

He lifted bent fingers to his face and rubbed his eyes. He wished the bed would stop moving. It was going from side to side and back and forth, like a canoe in choppy water.

"Quit shaking him," Rook told Chango. "That won't help."

"Cold water," Chango muttered. "I'll get some cold water."

"No," Rook said. "Cold water wouldn't do it. He ain't drunk. He's way past that. Been somewhere and got himself charged up. Or maybe it's like I figured, and he's the kind don't need no charge."

"Get him out of it," Chango ordered.

"Me?"

"Yeah." Chango's tone was impatient. "Go to work on him. Get him out of it."

"What the hell do I look like, a magician?"

Then it was quiet. He heard the heavy breathing of Chango and the hissing breathing of Rook. He couldn't hear his own breathing, and figured that maybe he wasn't breathing at all. He decided he might as well close his eyes; it just didn't pay to keep them open when they weren't working right. Everything was mixed up out there past the lenses, as though the eyeballs were seeing through a film of streaked mica.

He closed his eyes and right after that the iron chair gave way and he felt himself being lowered slowly, until once again he was flat on his back.

He heard the voice of Chango, thick and soft and somehow soothing, very close to his ear. "You didn't answer my question. Why'd you visit Pete Lanson? What'd you want to see him about?"

He heard it clearly, knew it was the voice of the huge man who was part Irish, part Chinese. But he couldn't take it past that. So he decided there was no use trying to reply.

Then someone's hand was working on the pockets of the raglan, going inside the raglan to play around with the pockets of his jacket and trousers.

"It ain't here," Rook said.

Chango's tone remained soft and soothing. "Tell me, pal, what'd you do with the knife?"

He wondered what the man was talking about. Suddenly he caught a glimpse of someone running through the snow and tossing a leather-sheathed hunting knife over the shoulder.

And he said, "I threw it away."

He heard the sound of fingers snapping, then Rook's voice: "There. You see? You get it?"

"Shut up," Chango said to Rook. Then, to Darby, "What happened at Lanson's? What'd you do?"

He wished the man would quit asking questions that were impossible to answer. What was this place they called Lanson's? Maybe they were just having fun with him and there was no such place. A couple of jokers, that's what they were. Well, live and let live. Let them have their fun.

The fingers snapped again. Rook said, "I'm ready to bet on it. He rubbed Lanson."

"Add it up," Chango said.

"Figure it this way. Just from what we saw with our own eyes. We saw him in the pawnshop, stealing the knife. He pays us off to keep it quiet. Then we follow him to Lanson's. We see him go in and then he and Lanson talk for a while and then Lanson puts the light out. We're out there on the street and we see a light go on upstairs. Twenty minutes, thirty minutes, and then it's dark upstairs but we don't see this guy coming out. And I'll tell you why. He got out the back way."

It was quiet again, until Rook said, "That store won't open up tomorrow."

"Too bad," Chango murmured mildly. "The place did a nice business."

Rook's laugh was squeaky. "Ever see the wrist watch?"

"What wrist watch?"

"Lanson's. Solid-gold case. Sapphires. I know the pure merchandise when I see it. One time I see him wearing a tie clasp with a green stone big as a jelly bean. I'll swear it was real."

Chango's voice dropped a few octaves. "You getting ideas?"

"Just playing around. Look at it. We know Lanson was a big spender. He only wore the best. So one and one makes two and it's a better angle than putting the squeeze on this charged-up nut. If Lanson don't have at least five grand worth of goods up there, I'll jump off the Delaware Bridge."

"Five grand," Chango mused.

"At the very least."

"What else is upstairs?"

"Just Lanson. No other tenants."

"That's pretty," Chango said.

Rook's tone was decisive. "It's a setup."

Chango grunted. Then he said, "How do we get in?"

"The way this guy got out. Through the back door." He added, "Won't be no problem at all. A cinch to handle the automatic lock. And the burglar alarm. My fingers ain't lost the gift."

Then a long pause.

Chango pondered, "Maybe Lanson's still alive." He waited for a rebuttal and, not getting any, went on, "These knife jobs are tricky. The man's on the floor and he ain't moving but he's breathing. So we come in and commence the heist. And he sees us."

"If that happens," Rook said, "it'll be complicated."

"I don't like these complications."

"All right, then," Rook said easily. "Let's forget about it."

Chango snorted. "Shut up for a minute. Let me think." Rook complied.

Presently Chango said, "If Lanson's still alive, I'll finish him."

Another long pause.

Then Rook said, "You ready?"

"Don't rush me."

"What bothers you now?"

"This guy here."

Darby felt something touching his ribs.

He heard the squeaky laugh again as Rook said, "This lunatic?"

"Don't sell him short," Chango warned.

"You kidding? He was made to order for this rap."

"We got to be sure he gets it. Here's what to do. Reach in his pocket. Take his wallet."

Rook lifted the wallet with a swift and easy motion
and handed it to Chango, who glanced briefly at the
driver's license and the social-security card and muttered,
"This is plenty. They'll find these cards in the room.
They'll have the case wrapped up before tomorrow
night."

But now it was Rook's turn to ponder. "I don't know
about that. When you take a knife and carve a man, you
don't open your wallet and toss your cards around."

"Oh, yes, you do," Chango said. "According to the
dicks, that's just the sort of trick you're apt to pull. When
you ain't in your right mind."

Rook let out the squeaky laugh. This time it was pure
admiration of the huge man's ability to build a job and
get past the hurdles, and he said, "It's peaches and cream,
Chango. It's perfect."

"Yeah," Chango murmured. "I think it's gonna be all
right."

Rook began to whistle a little tune that went up and
down the scale like a seesaw on wheels.

"Let's go," Chango said.

Rook got up off the edge of the bed, still whistling the
little up-and-down melody.

So then, in Darby's ears, there was the sound of the
tiny flute that hopped from one end of a seesaw to the
other. The sound was going away, along with the sound
of receding footsteps. Then he heard a door opening
down there. Or up there. In the dark gray distance.

He heard the door closing and smiled contentedly He
told himself that now everything was just fine, the visit-
ors had gone away and he was all alone and finally he'd
really get some sleep.

Gradually, as his eyes shut tighter, his smile became
a grimace.

Chapter 15

Deep in the forest there was a crystal pond, rimmed with sunflowers. Beyond that, the grass was not the color of grass at all, it was pale green. And the bark of the trees was orange, as though someone had come through here with a paintbrush. Suddenly there was the snarling of something vicious, and in the next moment they appeared, the pack of wild dogs showing their teeth. But they weren't on the ground. They were flying, and that was impossible, yet there they were, the dogs up there flying forward through the treetops; flying without wings.

He gasped, and looked for a place to hide. There was no place to hide and he ran frantically toward the crystal pond and leaped in. He saw the dogs flying down to get him and he surface-dived, forcing his way downward and telling himself they couldn't follow him down here. But then he heard the snarling, and turned his head and saw the dogs coming down through the water. He opened his mouth and let the flood come in, and hoped he would drown before the dogs got him. Now they were closing in, yet instead of staring at their approaching fangs, he was observing the color of their fur. It was platinum blonde.

Then the water was black and the dogs had vanished. The blackness was warm and the water tasted salty. He could feel himself rising slowly toward the surface and kept his eyes shut tightly until he felt the change from water to air.

The first thing he saw was the unshaded electric bulb dangling directly over the cot.

Then he heard the coughing from the other cots.

He sat up and looked around. Up there in front they were still grouped at the window, looking down on

Eighth Street. And down there at the far end the other
group was still busy with penny-ante poker. Between the
two groups the rows of cots were filled with sleeping
men and groaning men and men who were sitting up,
just like himself, wondering what to do next.

He looked at his wrist watch. Three-ten. Too late to
go home, so maybe the best thing to do was go back to
sleep. But now he wasn't at all tired.

It was strange. He hadn't slept very long, and he
ought to be very tired, especially with all that junk in
him, that snuff-aspirin-cola mixture.

He winced just then, wondering if Woodrow had returned the wallet.

He moved his hand and felt for the wallet and it
wasn't there. But in the same instant he distinctly remembered that Woodrow had returned it to him, and he
had handed Woodrow a five-dollar bill.

In the next instant he remembered Chango and Rook.

And somewhere in his brain a lever clicked and a wire
recorder began to play it back, the conversation he had
recorded without knowing he was doing it. It started at
the end, the whistling music, the little seesaw tune, and
made is way backward from there, with Chango saying,
"I think it's gonna be all right," and Rook saying, "This
lunatic?"

He could hear Chango saying, "If Lanson's still alive,
I'll finish him," and Rook saying, "Made to order for
this rap."

He was out of the cot and running down the aisle. He
opened the door and ran down the narrow hall past the
old man, who didn't even bother to look up from the
Greek newspaper.

He went leaping down the stairs to come sliding and
skidding as he hit the icy pavement along Eighth Street.
He told himself it was too late, it had happened already,
but still he ran, begging the street to show him a police
car, or a policeman, or anyone to whom he could shout
for aid. But all the street showed was a mongrel under a
corner lamp, unsteady on four shivering legs, trying to
make up its mind between three garbage cans.

As Darby lunged across Vine, a big truck came rumbling toward him and he jumped out of the way, waving frantically to the driver. The driver grinned and waved cheerily and the truck whizzed past.

He cursed himself for having failed to rouse the old man from the Greek newspaper. He should have thought of that. Or enlisting the aid of the men on the cots. There were a lot of things he should have thought about.

He had never seen a street that looked so empty.

The mouth of the alley beside the drugstore was wide open, saying, come on, come on, and he entered the gap between a splintered fence and brick walls, wondering what kept him upright and traveling so fast when the hard-packed snow was so slippery. He streaked down the alley and came to the door that was open just a little. He opened it wider, and just as he darted in, he heard the sound of fighting upstairs.

There were no voices, just some bumping and thudding. As he started up the stairway he heard the sound of a chair hitting the floor. But all at once every sound was stopped, even the sound of his own feet on the stairs. And he was telling himself to do it very quiet, go on from here with caution and cunning, so they wouldn't be prepared for his arrival.

At least, he told himself as he moved noiselessly down the hall, there was that one chance. If he could take them by surprise, and if there was enough dismay, they might discard the project entirely and just get the hell out as fast as they could.

But of course it was too late, and he bit hard at his lip and wished he could stop thinking it was too late.

He came to the closed door of the bedroom. He turned the knob and opened the door and managed it with hardly any sound.

He saw Rook busy at a chest of drawers, all the drawers open and Rook's fingers stabbing in and out. He saw an overturned lamp and an overturned chair and Chango straddling the motionless form of Pete Lanson. Chango's arms were rigid, sending pressure through the wrists and into the thick fingers around Pete's throat.

As Darby leaped at Chango, there was a warning yell from Rook, and Chango turned and tried to rise. Darby swung wide with his right arm and his fist caught Chango in the eye. The huge man fell sideways and Darby aimed a kick at him and missed. Then he whirled in time to dodge the bronze book end that Rook was using as a club. Rook tried again with the book end and Darby went inside the flashing bronze arc, chopped with his right hand, and caught Rook flush on the point of the jaw. Rook went to his knees, fell on his face, and stayed flat on the floor.

Chango was up and coming at Darby, the fingers spread wide and clutching. Darby threw an overhand right that was wild, and Chango snatched at the wrist, missed, and took Darby's left hook just under the ear. He grinned at Darby and came moving in.

Darby looked down, saw the bronze book end, and made a grab for it, but he wasn't quick enough. Chango caught him, lifted him up, and went on lifting him until he was held almost horizontal above Chango's head.

Chango hurled him across the room, aiming him at the wall.

But he landed on the bed, and came up very fast as Chango lunged again. He kicked Chango in the face. Chango just stood there for a moment, studying him while allowing two teeth to fall out of a bleeding mouth. Then Chango's head was lowered and he dived in low, his arms circling Darby's knees. The two of them went sailing back across the bed, hitting the floor with Chango on top.

Chango put his hands around Darby's throat and began to squeeze.

Just then Rook came to his senses, stood up, saw what was happening, and cried, "No, don't do that! You do away with him and we lose the fall guy."

Chango's mouth popped open. "You're right. I wasn't even thinking."

"Just knock him out," Rook said.

Chango took his hands away from Darby's throat. Slowly and with considerable enjoyment he closed his right

hand and tightened the knuckles, taking careful aim at
Darby's chin. Darby jerked his head to the side, at the
same instant reaching up with both hands and grab-
bing handfuls of Chango's thick black hair. He pulled
with all his might.

The room was torn with Chango's scream of shock
and pain. Darby, still pulling at the black strands,
squirmed out from beneath the huge man, heard a
strange wet ripping sound that seemed to come from
Chango's scalp, and got past the scream. Now Chango
was on his knees, his palms flat on the floor, while Darby
stood above him and tugged at the hair.

Rook didn't move. He had never seen anything quite
like this and he stood there in the grip of terror mixed
with fascination. He saw the blood squirting from Chango's scalp, heard the ripping sound getting louder, and
all at once the complete ripping as a portion of the scalp
came away.

Chango was going crazy with pain. He fell on his side
and rolled over on his back and had his eyes shut tightly as he shook his fists at the ceiling.

The dark green broadloom was blotched with hair
and tissue and blood.

It was a little too much for Rook. He saw the same
thing happening to himself, and he let out a yelp and
made for the door. Chango leaped up, let out a final
scream that became a sob, and followed Rook out of the
room. The sound of Chango's sobbing trailed back
through the hall, then died away altogether.

Darby sat down on the edge of the bed. He wanted to
take a look at Pete Lanson. He was afraid to look at
Pete.

He saw the wallet on the floor and the cards scattered
around. He told himself the only thing to do was put
the cards back in the wallet and put the wallet in his
pocket and get out of here while the getting was good.

He picked up the cards and the wallet and moved toward the door.

But somehow that didn't seem fair.

He wondered why the hell he was thinking in terms

of fair and unfair, or right and wrong, or any conception of the good thing to do as opposed to the bad thing. The night was ending as he had wanted it to end, with the stillness there on the floor on the other side of the bed, the conclusive evidence that Lover Boy would never again make love. So the wish had been realized and now it was all over.

He was trying very hard to make himself believe that it was all over while he turned away from the door and moved slowly toward the other side of the bed.

He heard the groan that meant that Pete was still alive; he did not hear his own deep sigh of relief and thanks.

It was thirty minutes later and Pete was seated in a chair near the window, his bared throat shiny with thick white ointment that concealed the bluish marks. Darby leaned against the window sill, smoking a cigarette.

Without apology or regret or any emotion at all, he had told Pete everything, starting from four years back, the wedding-day incident, then leaping to the incident of several nights ago, when Vivian had pretended to call the police, and taking it forward from there. Pete sat and stared at the floor and didn't make a single interruption.

Now it was finished and he waited for Pete to say something.

It appeared that Pete had nothing to say, and finally Darby murmured, "I think I'm able to handle it now. If she really wants you, I'll get out of the way."

Pete looked at him. "You actually believe it, don't you?"

"There's nothing else I can believe."

"There's plenty," Pete said. He put his hand to the side of his neck and gave a little cough. "You're a sick man, Al. You're very sick."

Darby opened his mouth to deny that, and discovered that he couldn't build a contradiction.

"No matter what I tell you," Pete said, "you won't buy

it. You trust me as far as you can throw a ten-ton truck. Not only me. Everyone. It's written all over your face."

From where he was standing, he could see his face in the dresser mirror. It didn't seem as though there were anything wrong with his expression. His face was quite calm, he was even smiling just a little.

He murmured, "I wish you'd explain that wedding-day deal. Or maybe you'll tell me you don't remember."

"I remember," Pete said. "What you overheard was an argument involving money, nothing else."

He frowned. "Money?"

"Her father had loaned me a couple of hundred dollars. She thought I was trying to beat the debt." He added, with a mild indignation, "Inside of a month it was all straightened out."

He wondered what he could say to that, knowing there was nothing he could say. His silence was a complete acceptance of Pete's statement.

"Anything else?" Pete asked gently.

He shook his head. And just to do something, he moved away from the window sill and picked up some socks and handkerchiefs that were scattered on the floor. He put them back in the opened drawers of the dresser.

He said, "I hope they didn't take anything."

Pete laughed lightly. "I looked. All they got was a pair of cuff links. Worth about three dollars."

Darby picked up some neckties and folded them and put them in the drawer. "Better see about that throat. Better call your doctor."

"I'll go see him tomorrow," Pete said. He stood up and his smile was friendly and forgiving, and he put a hand on Darby's shoulder. "Al, I hope you'll be all right. Whatever it is, I hope you clear it up."

Darby's eyes were looking in the mirror and seeing a puzzle. "Whatever it is."

He saw the floor and the walls in a pale green blur, like the depths of a misted forest from which there was no exit, even though he was opening a door.

He said good-by to Pete and walked out of the room and deeper into the forest.

Chapter 16

ON VINE STREET he climbed into a taxi and some forty minutes later he arrived home. All the lights were out, and as he entered the house he told himself to walk quietly and let her sleep. He went into the bedroom and saw the mass of dark hair on the pillow and heard the soft steady rhythm of her breathing. He was very anxious to talk to her, but he decided it wouldn't be fair to wake her up at this time of night.

He carried a robe and flannel pajamas into the bathroom, sent hot water running into the tub, stepped in, and rubbed soap onto a sponge. The water was very hot and at first it was an ordeal, but gradually he felt the steaming luxury of it and told himself it was sort of nice to be home again.

He climbed out of the tub and dried himself and lathered his face and shaved. It was really very nice to be home. He put on his slippers and tightened the belt of the robe. Then he went into the kitchen and put coffee on the stove.

He was sitting at the table, sipping coffee and taking drags at a cigarette, when something caused him to lift his head, and he saw Vivian in the doorway.

"Hello," he said.

She didn't answer. She came into the kitchen and took a cup and saucer from the cupboard and poured some coffee for herself. She stood there at the stove, sipping the coffee.

He said, "I'm sorry if I woke you up."

"You didn't wake me up," she told him. "I heard you come in."

"You did?" He lit another cigarette. "Then why'd you make out you were sleeping?"

145

"I wanted to see what you'd do."

He puffed hard at the cigarette. "What did you think I'd do?"

She shrugged and said lightly, "Oh, I just thought you'd pack your things and write a farewell note."

The cigarette tasted bitter. He started to kill it, then changed his mind and took another hard puff. "What gave you that idea?"

She brought her coffee to the table and sat down. "I don't know," she murmured. "Maybe it's what I want you to do."

He frowned. "You mean you really want me to do that?" The cigarette dropped to the floor. His hands were like pliers biting at the edge of the table. "You want me to go away?"

She turned the cup this way and that way in the saucer. "I'm not sure," she said. "The way I feel right now, I'm not sure what I want you to do."

He bent down and picked up the cigarette. He said, "I suppose you're pretty fed up with me."

"I am."

It hurt, but he smiled and kept his eyes on the cigarette and said, "And you don't want me any more?"

"No."

"I don't believe you," he said.

"Don't you?" Her laugh was dry and brief. "Just what do you expect me to do—throw myself at your knees and beg? You think I'm one of these damn-fool women who throws herself on the bed and cries her eyes out? It might interest you to know I went out tonight and enjoyed myself."

"Really?" he murmured. "That's nice."

For a long moment she just sat there and looked at him. Her lips were tight and she was breathing hard. And then she was breathing harder. And suddenly she leaped up and grabbed the coffee cup and hurled it at his head.

The cup grazed the side of his head and went sailing past and crashed against the wall. Some coffee splattered on his shoulder.

He didn't move. His voice was relaxed. "What was that for?"

"For being so goddamn clever," she seethed. She started toward him. "Where were you tonight? Who were you with?"

"Now, wait—"

"Wait, nothing." She closed in on him and snatched the cigarette from his lips. "And don't give me any fairy tales. Just tell me why your eyes are bloodshot, and where you got that scratch on your cheek. Go on, tell me all about the wild party. What was her name?"

Hovering over him, she had hold of his shoulders. He tried to get up from the chair, but her weight pressed him back against the wall.

"Quit crowding me," he said.

"Tell me her name."

"Lay off, will you?" He made another attempt to squirm free, but she held him there.

She shouted, "You'll tell me her name. I'll make you tell me—"

"Stop broadcasting," he pleaded. "The neighbors—"

"The hell with the neighbors." Her face was flushed. Her eyes were wild.

He told himself it was nothing very much out of the ordinary. It was just another married couple having a row late at night. And certainly it wasn't the first time he'd battled with her. So it really wasn't anything to worry about and the best way to handle it was just to let her carry on and raise the roof until she got tired.

She was shouting and calling him names, but he wasn't paying attention. He was telling himself there were far worse situations than sitting in the kitchen and facing an angry wife, especially a wife who looked so pretty when she was angry. It was really exciting to have her so near, as she held him down in the chair. She was calling him a dirty no-good cheating sonofabitch and he was concentrating on the ripe and juicy fullness of her body underneath the nightgown.

He told himself this was some woman, really terrific. Maybe he could talk her into sitting on his lap.

"You filthy sneak," she blazed. "Why'd you bother
to come home at all? Just to take a bath? And don't sit
there grinning. Don't grin at me, damn you."

He sat there eating her up with his eyes, and felt the
hot craving racing through him as she came in closer
and shook him viciously.

"I said don't grin at me."

He reached out and put his arms around her middle.

She pulled away violently. He came up from the chair
and made another grab at her. He caught a flap of the
nightgown and somehow he couldn't let go and the fabric ripped and went on ripping and still he couldn't let
go.

The grin was lazy and yet his eyes were determined.

He had hold of the nightgown with both hands and
he was tearing it from her shoulders. She stared at him
blankly, and for a moment her eyes said, This is someone I don't know. But in the next moment her eyes
flamed with rage, and she slapped him with all her
might across the mouth.

He fell backward and hit the table and held onto it for
support.

But the grin remained on his lips as he mumbled,
"Crazy about you, really I am. I'm just crazy about you."

She was working with the shreds of the nightgown,
trying to cover her nakedness.

He moved toward her. She stepped backward and
said, "Keep away from me."

She continued to move backward. He advanced slowly.

She retreated all the way down the hall and into the
bedroom. She tried to close the door in his face, but he
forced his way in. She ran to the dresser and picked up
a large hand mirror.

"I'm warning you," she said. "Keep away."

"What for?" he asked mildly, as though he had no
idea what all the fuss was about. "Didn't you hear me
telling you? I said I was crazy about you."

"All right," she said. "Thanks a lot. Now get out."

She gestured with the hand mirror, indicating the
door. He stared at the door as though he didn't know

what it was. "What do you mean, get out? Where do you want me to go?"

"I don't care where you go. Just get out."

His head was clearing. He could feel the floor, solid and all too real, under his feet. The grin was gone now and his face was expressionless as he said, "This is where I live."

"Really?" she said. "It's nice of you to tell me. I wouldn't have known."

He bit hard at the corner of his mouth. "And I wasn't with a woman tonight."

She put the hand mirror on the dresser and said quietly, "Will you swear to that?"

"You have my word," he said. "If it'll help matters any, I'll make it a solemn oath. Since the day of our marriage I haven't put my hands on any woman except you."

She sat down on the edge of the bed. She looked at the floor. "Maybe you're telling the truth. I wish I could be sure. There's something—something I don't understand." She took a deep breath, and then went on. "The other night, when you thought you heard a burglar, and I said I'd call the police. I didn't call the police. I made that phone call to my father."

He didn't say anything.

She went on looking at the floor. "I called my father because I needed someone to confide in. Someone I could trust. I was afraid. For both of us. I've phoned him many times late at night. I've seen him during the day." She raised her head, and her eyes were calm. "I've been telling him about what's been happening between you and me. And all he does is sit there and nod. And tells me I shouldn't worry about it."

"Why don't you follow his advice?"

Her smile was dim and sort of weary. "I've tried. I've tried as hard as I could. But somehow I just can't get rid of the feeling."

"What do you mean? What feeling?"

"I keep telling myself there's someone else." She stood up. The smile faded and she was pressing her lips tightly to keep them from trembling. And then she said, "It's true, isn't it? You have another woman on your mind."

He turned away.

He felt her hand on his shoulder and heard her saying, "Tell me. Please tell me. Who is she?"

He lowered his head and stared at the floor and wished he could sink through it. He said, "I can't tell you."

Her hand fell away from his shoulder. There was a moment of hollow stillness.

"I'm sorry," he said. "I just can't talk about it."

"Why not?" She took hold of him and turned him around, forced him to face her. "What are you afraid of?"

He was breathing hard, as though breathing were a painful effort. As though the air were seeping out of the room, and if he didn't run away from here he would suffocate.

He couldn't look at her.

She pleaded, "What is it? Why do you look so guilty? Tell me."

He felt her arms around him. But there was no warmth, no rapture, it was like the pressure of chains, trying to hold him here in the suffocating chamber.

He pushed her away, and smiled thinly at this dark-haired girl who wore a torn nightgown and watched him while he got dressed. She followed him from the room and down the hall, and watched him as he put on the raglan and the muffler and watched him from the kitchen window as he backed the Plymouth out of the garage.

The frozen streets aimed at nowhere. And Frankford wasn't Frankford at all, just a cold and dark and empty land where lamps glowed here and there and didn't throw light on anything. The Plymouth moved slowly around and around in a circle that crossed Roosevelt Boulevard just east of Castor Avenue, and came up to cross it again several blocks west of Castor Avenue. There was no traffic to disturb the route, and the Plymouth rode around and around.

He knew he was driving an automobile that wasn't taking him anywhere, but that didn't matter. Because every now and then he'd close his eyes and in the blackness he'd drift away from the automobile, from everything, and he'd see the black screen, and then the face.

The face of a girl. And her hair was platinum blonde.

And every time he looked at her, he came closer. So that finally the features were clear and he knew who she was.

The girl was fifteen years old. She was Marjorie. She was his sister.

And he stood there, the kid brother. A grim-faced boy of twelve, with a suitcase in his hand.

He was saying good-by to Marjorie. Saying it very quietly because it was very late at night and of course he didn't want to wake his parents.

Marjorie wasn't trying to stop him. She shivered just a little, but only because it was so cold down here in the living room near the front door. She had her hands in the pockets of her bathrobe as she said, "Where will you go?"

"I don't know."

"You got any money?"

He nodded.

She said, "Aren't you afraid to go away by yourself?"

"No," he said. "I ain't afraid."

Then, not looking at him, and sort of forcing it out, she said, "You know, you really don't have to do this. Nobody's making you go."

He wondered why she said it that way—almost as if she wanted him to go. He couldn't understand why she wasn't looking at him. After all, this was their last moment together. They'd never see each other again.

Tears flooded his eyes and poured down his face. Not because he was running away from home. Only because he couldn't bear the thought of leaving Marjorie.

Yet his grip was determined on the handle of the suitcase. With his other hand he wiped the tears from his eyes. He opened the door and walked out of the house, to tremble then as he faced the dark and unknown world.

Of course it didn't last long. Six days, to be exact. He was vastly relieved when they brought him home. But the relief gave way to agony when he discovered that Marjorie wasn't there. And his parents acted so strange. They hardly talked to him at all. They merely told him that Marjorie had been sent away to live with relatives in the country, as though that was the end of it and there must be no further talk about it. The thing had happened and it was ended.

The Plymouth was crossing Roosevelt Boulevard. He was trying to come back from eighteen years ago, but a hook shaped like a question mark refused to let him come all the way back.

Why had he run away from home when he was twelve years old?

What had he done?

He groped for the answer, and was scarcely aware that he had the Plymouth aiming toward Kensington.

Toward the pale green eyes and platinum-blonde hair of Geraldine.

Chapter 17

A T FIVE-FIFTEEN in the morning a blizzard came screeching through Kensington, and within a few minutes it had reached its full force. On Allegheny Avenue a streetcar was knocked off the tracks and went lunging into a stalled milk truck that fell on its side and narrowly missed Darby's Plymouth. It would have hit the Plymouth if Darby hadn't pulled very hard at the wheel and driven the car into a hill of snow. He backed it off, circled the entanglement of streetcar and milk truck, and felt the car quivering as the wind tried to roll it off its wheels. In front of the windshield the air and the street were blended to become a white whirlpool of snow.

The car turned a corner, then turned a few more corners and made its way up the narrow street and came to a grinding stop outside the house that had once been a candy shop.

He got out of the car and went up to the door and rang the bell. He thought it would take at least two or three minutes of ringing the bell to get her waked up, but just a few moments after the first ring the door opened and he was looking at the platinum-blonde hair and the cheap fur coat and the low-heeled slippers.

She wasn't looking at him. She gazed past his head, out at the white stampede of wind and snow.

Then she turned, beckoning him to come on in and close the door. As he followed her in, he saw the orange glow down there in the back room where the electric burner was trying to warm the house. He caught the fragrance of the Japanese perfume and saw the languid flow of the squirrel pelts, the fur coat sort of luxurious and elegant even though it was old and torn.

In the back room she took off the squirrel and he saw

that same gray dress she had been wearing on the night so long ago. Or was it only last night?

He said, "I'm sorry I woke you up."

She walked to the couch and sat down and smiled at him. "I wasn't sleeping."

Darby frowned. "At this hour? What were you doing?"

"Just sitting here," she murmured. "Waiting for you."

He took off the raglan and folded it over a chair. "How'd you know I'd be back?"

"I just knew, that's all." Then suddenly she was sitting up rigid and staring at him and saying, "What the hell are you looking at?"

"Your hair."

Instinctively she raised a hand to her head. "What's wrong with my hair?"

"Nothing," he said. "It looks very nice."

She shrugged. "It's the same as it always was. You've seen it before."

"Have I?" He was moving toward the couch. "No, I don't think so. Or maybe I didn't take notice. I didn't appreciate how pretty it really is."

"Is that why you drove your car through a blizzard? Just to look at my pretty hair?"

He sat down on the couch beside her. "I came here to be with you."

She lifted her hands close to her eyes and carefully examined the orange fingernails. She ran her thumbs across the glossy enamel, breathing slowly in a sort of quiet pleasure, as though the air in the room tasted good.

And she said, still studying the fingernails, "You better think it over. You're taking a big chance."

"Why?"

She looked at him. Her smile was dim. "I guess I should have told you. I have a boy friend."

For a moment he felt nothing. Then all at once he was cold with jealousy. Before he could try to reason it out, the anger showed in his eyes and his voice. "I don't think I like that."

"I didn't expect that you would." And she was leaning back, looking him up and down with a mild appraisal, then nodding slightly, satisfied with whatever she saw.

Darby sat tensely, his fists on his knees. "What's the man's name?"

She widened her eyes just a little. "Really," she said, "I don't think that's any of your business."

"It is."

The blunt way he said it caused her eyebrows to go up. But the dim smile stayed there on her lips. Then the shrug again. "Oh, well, if you feel that way about it. His name is Charlie."

"Charlie." He heard himself spitting out the name as though it were venom. "How long have you known this Charlie?"

He saw her sitting back with her head relaxed against the velours, her eyes looking straight ahead now, the smile still dim but somehow changed, sort of aiming away from the room. "About a year."

"You've known me longer than that."

"So?" She continued to look straight ahead. "What does that mean?"

He opened his mouth to blurt a reply and discovered there was no reply. He struggled with it for a few moments and couldn't do anything with it and finally said, "All right, tell me. What about this Charlie? What goes on?"

"He's nice."

"Goddamn it!" The fury sizzled, and he heard the hissing of his breath and stood up and walked across the room and came back to the couch. He couldn't say anything.

"Yes," Geraldine breathed. "Charlie's very nice. And he's always here when I want him."

"Now, listen," Darby said. "You cut that out. What are you trying to do, stir me up?"

"You're stirred up already." She inclining her head with the dim smile still there. "I'm just wondering what you're going to do about it."

"Push him aside, that's what."

"You really think you can manage it?"

"Damn right."

She let out the dry little laugh. "But look, Alvin. Look at it this way. Charlie's a steady situation. He's here almost every day. You visit me once every six years."

Darby stared at the platinum-blonde hair. "It hasn't been six years. Hasn't even been an hour. I never went away."

Then all he heard was the quiet. And all he saw was the platinum-blonde hair and the pale green eyes. Coming toward him, even though she hadn't moved. And the breasts coming toward him, the orange fingernails playing idly with white buttons to loosen the flap of the dress. The Japanese perfume floated into his head. And just then, as he felt the flame rising and felt the thickness in his throat, the tingling in every pore, he saw the front of the dress falling away, and her hands cupped there underneath the naked breasts, the silent invitation.

And her mouth was open. The tip of her tongue was sliding slowly back and forth across the orange lipstick. The pale green eyes smiled at him as he came toward her, and without seeming to move she arranged herself on the couch. The flame inside him was volcanic, the crest of it exploding in his brain as he saw her arms coming up toward him, felt her hands on his face, then tasted her mouth.

The clothes that fell to the floor piece by piece were like segments of time dropping away, taking him back and back and far back to the nights added onto nights; the long-ago total of nights on this same couch, when they had soared together up somewhere on a star far away from Kensington and Philadelphia and all the living world. On a star where the fire scorched but never pained, where they had their own special way of making fire.

And now he heard her saying, "You never kissed me like that before."

He breathed, "Geraldine," while the blizzard sent one of its battalions through the narrow gap of the alley outside and the wind howled against the window.

The skin of Geraldine was white magic that sent the blizzard away and put out the light in the room even though the bulb was still lit. Through the strange dark-gray mist he saw the orange face of the electric burner. It moved around and around and then it went away altogether, but suddenly it came back and the glowing wires touched his chest. He looked down and saw her fingernail biting into his chest, the slow circling journey that caused his flesh to give way and the blood to show. And then it was there again, the red G.

Her eyes told him to come on, kiss her again. Kiss her here. And here. And take the hands away from there and put them here. Oh, it's wonderful, it's like nothing that ever happened before. Like climbing up and down on a lightning bolt, that's what it's like.

Her breasts were stones against his chest and her breath came in slow dragging gasps and her head began to roll from side to side, as her eyes shut tightly with the unbearably delicious pain.

And then the lapse of six years became a greater lapse, the star came shooting out across a void in which there was no such thing as measured space or a knowledge of time. There was nothing at all except the throbbing and the flame, no record of anything, no memory, no idea. The star was traveling beyond the limit of understood speed, going even faster than that, so fast that it didn't seem to be moving at all. Then all at once it wasn't a star any more. It was a garden where the flame had quieted down, like melted gold getting cooled to take the shape of a golden flower.

He looked at the platinum-blonde hair and heard Geraldine saying, "Now you're mine again. And this time you won't get away."

She was looking at the red G carved on his chest.

"You're mine," she said, and her voice was a hook that caught him and held him and pulled him away from sleep. They were in the bedroom and it was a few minutes past seven in the morning. He heard the gnashing and shrieking of the blizzard outside, and saw, through the window, the snow heaped several inches above the sill. He lifted his head from the pillow and felt Geraldine's arms around him, felt the countless petals of the wild flower, her warm flesh pressed all along the length of his body.

The pale green eyes said, This is the way it is, Alvin. You and Geraldine. From here on in. There's nothing else, no other law, no other thought. You know it, don't you? Of course you know it. Of course you know it.

So then again it was the lightning flash, the high voltage. It was up there on the flaming star millions of miles above the earth of this world.

Her eyes were demanding and commanding and smiling at him and daring him to say no. And his eyes were all surrender, all worship, so her smile was wider and she nodded slowly.

Her legs were scissors of fire. Her arms were flexible iron, letting him know she controlled everything, even the flow of blood in his veins.

The pale green eyes said, You've been away a long time. Now you'll make up for it.

The blizzard shrieked louder and she cried, "Oh, darling! Darling!"

Then it was like crawling through a furnace, in the depths of the orange glow, down and down to where the fire was hottest.

Then there was her wailing laugh that climbed and climbed until it broke and her arms and legs were limp and her eyes were closed.

The small clock on the table said seven-thirty. He knew he'd better be getting up and getting dressed and going to work. Then he thought of the snowstorm and saw a picture of blocked traffic and people waiting for streetcars and busses that wouldn't arrive, and most of them saying the hell with it and going back home.

He smiled at the pleasant picture of all the people going back home and getting under the quilts, and fell asleep.

"Coffee?" she said. "You hungry? You want something?"

It was three in the afternoon and she had just waked

up, and waked him up. Beyond the window, the alley
was a tube filled with ice. The snow was still coming
down. The wind had quieted a little and now the snow
fell in an almost solid white mass, an unwavering oblique
path.

"Just coffee," he said.

She got out of bed and went out of the room. She
came back and told him the coffee can was empty. He
said it didn't matter, he could do without coffee.

"Really?" Her eyes narrowed. "What about me?"

"All right," he said. "I'll run out and get some."
He went into the bathroom to get washed, but she came
in and turned off the faucet.

"You'll do that later," she said. "I want the coffee
right away."

He walked into the bedroom and put on his clothes.
Geraldine said she wanted a cigarette. He gave her one
and took one for himself.

He buttoned up the raglan and started out of the bedroom, but turned in the doorway to ask, "Where's the
nearest store?"

"Right around the corner. On Kensington Avenue."

He went out and down the hall toward the front door.
He was about to open the front door when she called to
him from the bedroom.

"What is it?" he called back.

"Come here and I'll tell you."

He went back to the bedroom and saw Geraldine
standing at the dresser and looking in the mirror.

"Listen," she said. "I like a certain kind of coffee."
She told him the name of the brand. It was a foreign-
sounding name and he said he had never heard of it,
And Geraldine said, "Yes, it's hard to get. Only special
stores carry it. You can't buy it around here. You'll have
to go down to South Philly."

He frowned. Even in fair weather it was a good forty-
minute ride to South Philadelphia.

Geraldine said, "The store's around Sixth and Dickinson."

In the mirror he saw her looking at him, waiting for

him to voice the entirely reasonable objection. Daring
him to utter the slightest sound of complaint.

All he said was: "Hope I can get the car started."

"If you can't," she murmured, "just take a taxi."

He went out and saw immediately that even if he did
get the car started, he wouldn't be able to budge it.
There was too much snow. It was pressed hard against
the fenders. He walked up to Kensington Avenue and
had to stand on the corner for twenty minutes before a
taxi came along.

At five-thirty he returned with the coffee. He hadn't
found the brand she'd named in the vicinity of Sixth
and Dickinson and he'd lost count of all the stores he'd
walked into before he finally got the brand.

As he told her about it, she was taking the can from
the bag. She waited until he was finished, then looked
at the label and said, "You're a complete moron. You
know what you did? You brought the wrong coffee."

"What?" He stared at the label. "That's what you told
me to get."

"Did I?" She was imitating the weakness of his tone.
Then her voice was harsh and grinding. "Take it back."
She shoved the coffee can at him. "Go on, take it back
and bring me the kind I want."

"You go to hell."

She drew back her hand and made it into a fist and hit
him in the mouth. He tasted the blood and saw the color
of it in front of his eyes and decided it was appropriate
right now to haul off and clip her on the jaw.

Instead, he just stood there tasting the blood. The red
glare went away and he was staring at the platinum-
blonde hair.

She turned away and walked out of the room. He heard
her moving around in the kitchen, and he wanted to go
in and tell her he was sorry about the coffee. She was
absolutely right, and he'd been a complete moron to forget the name of the brand. But good God, how could he
have forgotten a simple little thing like the name of a
certain coffee? It just didn't seem possible he was that
stupid. Or maybe he was in some kind of fog and she'd

punched him in the mouth to snap him out of it. He began to develop the notion that the punch in the mouth was exactly what he deserved.

He went into the bathroom and put cold water in his mouth, squished it around, and looked at it as it flowed out pink. Then he looked in the mirror of the medicine cabinet and saw the slight bulge where the lip was cut on the inside to swell slightly on the outside. Exactly what he deserved.

Geraldine called to him and he entered the kitchen and saw the coffee bubbling in the glass top of the percolator. Then he looked at the sink and saw a mess of unwashed dishes. The garbage tray was heaped to overflowing and some of it had spilled over the side of the sink. It was apparent that the floor hadn't been scrubbed or even swept for days and days. The top of the kitchen table was stained with dried juices and gravies.

"Reach in the icebox," Geraldine said. "There's a jar of anchovies."

He opened the icebox. The only food in there was the jar of anchovies and part of a loaf of white bread.

She saw him gazing at the starved interior of the icebox, and said, "Don't stand there. Get the food."

"There isn't much of it."

"I don't require much." Then she added quickly, "Anyway, when I feel like a banquet, Charlie feeds me."

He decided he wouldn't answer that. Not right now. Quietly he suggested it might be a good idea to clean up the kitchen a little before they sat down to eat. She said if he wanted the kitchen clean, he could go ahead and clean it. She stood there leaning against the wall and smoking a cigarette while he used a broom and a rag and opened the back door and took the garbage out. When he came back in, expecting to see her at the sink washing the dishes, she hadn't moved from the wall. He shrugged and went to work on the dishes.

"If you like to do that," Geraldine told him, "I'll let you do it all the time."

"I'm only doing it because it's got to be done. Every room in this place needs cleaning."

"You calling me a slob?"

"I'm only saying—"

"Oh, shut up, shut up. Don't start boring me. I can't stand it when I'm bored."

He finished with the dishes and then they sat down to have the coffee and the bread and the anchovies. Geraldine lit another cigarette and smoked constantly while she ate. She told him to get up and pour her another cup of coffee.

As he poured the coffee, he heard her saying, "You know something? I like to be waited on. I just love it."

He poured a second cup for himself and sat down. The coffee was very strong and sort of thick and had a unique flavor. He saw she was enjoying it, and so of course this was the brand she'd told him to get. But he wasn't inclined to bring up the issue. He was anxious to discuss something much more important, the Charlie issue.

But before he could start it, he heard Geraldine saying, "That's what I want you to do all the time. Wait on me. Make out I'm the Queen of Arabia. You know what I'd like to have? I'd like a pair of them Arabian slippers, you know, the kind that turn up at the toes. And go around for days wearing a veil. Make out we're living in a tent in the desert. With camels all around. And the servants out there. Doing whatever I tell them. Don't care what it is, they've got to do what I say. Some nights I get bored. I get so bored I walk up and down and up and down. It's terrible. But you know what? In Arabia I won't let myself get bored. Oh, no. When I feel it coming on I'll walk outside the tent and clap my hands. Call one of the men. That's the way it'll be."

Darby said, "Listen, I want to ask you something."

"Wait." She held up a finger. "Let me go on with this Arabia kick. Now take the food, for instance. I read once they eat a lot of figs. So that's what you'll do, you'll go out and buy boxes and boxes of figs. Another thing they eat is lamb. But the hell with that, I can't stand lamb, no matter how it's fixed. Look, Alvin, here's what I want you to do right now. Go out and get me some figs."

She was sitting up very straight, her hands clasping the

edge of the table. Her eyes were extremely bright. She was breathing hard.

Then she shouted it. "Goddamn you, don't sit there. Didn't you hear what I said?"

"My God," he murmured. "What's wrong with you?"

Her features went through a slow contortion that made the face almost hideous. "You know what's wrong with me, you rotten filthy bastard."

Then she was up from the table and coming toward him and he leaped up and snatched at her wrists as she raised her clenched hands. He took hold of her wrists and twisted as hard as he could. She tried to kick him, and he jumped to the side and knew the situation needed something drastic, so he went on twisting her wrists until she was forced to her knees.

"Let go," she yelled. "Let go so I can do what I should have done six years ago. Rip your face apart. Tear your eyes out." She opened her mouth very wide and yowled like a cat. "You think I forgot about it? You think I let it pass, just like that? The way you ran out on me, after making a solemn promise we'd be married. What did you expect, that I'd forgive and forget?"

He knew he had to hold onto her wrists. If he let go, there was no telling what would happen. Even now, held down as she was, she twisted and kicked and he had all he could do to keep her on the floor.

"Your fault," she screeched. "You ruined everything for me. From the day you walked out I started going down the hill."

He didn't know what she meant by going down the hill. But he wasn't in the mood to start wondering about it. It seemed that her fury was of little importance compared to the rising anger he now felt within himself.

He released her wrists and stepped back, his eyes cold. "Get up," he said. "And you'd better calm yourself. You're liable to wind up getting hurt."

Her eyes showed that she believed him. Her eyes were wide and she was shaking her head slowly. Then she was up from the floor and leaning against the table, still staring at him.

His lips were tight and twisted. "You four-star phony. If I hadn't come back, you wouldn't know I was alive."

"That isn't true."

"Isn't it?" He heard the whispered trembling of his voice. "Then why did you wait? For six years you just sat here, waiting. Is that what you want me to believe?"

"Yes," she hissed at him. "Yes. Yes." She came toward him, her face the color of milk. "I knew you'd come back. Six years. Sixteen years. So what? Just a question of time. So I waited."

And now, all at once, he wasn't quite sure what was happening here, and he said, "What for?"

There was no hesitation. "To have you the way I've got you now. For the rest of my life."

"You really want that?" He hoped feverishly that was what she wanted. Because that was what he wanted. All of it. All the time. Beyond the wanting of the flesh, he wanted the Arabian queen who ruled without mercy, who demanded the fantastic and the downright impossible. Who gave him poison to drink and made him like it. And most of all he wanted this portrait constantly in front of his vision, the pale green eyes and the platinum-blonde hair.

"Yes," she said. "I want you, Alvin. Nothing else."

So now he knew it was going to happen. And he decided that it had to happen all the way. No side angles. No deviations. He let her know he wasn't going to miss a single trick as he sneered, "Not even Charlie?"

He expected, of course, that Charlie would now be cancelled out, that she would admit Charlie meant nothing, just another Kensington corner lounger who'd seen her walking down the street and decided to follow her and so was lured in to become nothing more than an errand boy.

He heard her saying, "No, I won't get rid of Charlie."

It was a cudgel, hitting him in the face. He couldn't say anything.

"You see," she said, "I like Charlie. I'm really very fond of Charlie."

And still he couldn't say anything.

"It's like this." Geraldine smiled softly. "I just can't live without Charlie."

His mouth moved without making sound. Then, when he was able to speak, he couldn't get it above a whisper. "What the hell is this? What kind of deal are you trying to pull?"

"No deal." The smile remained soft. "Just an arrangement, that's all. You'll belong to me. And I'll belong to Charlie."

His hand came up very slowly, the fingers drifting along the side of his head, while his eyes stared at a wall papered with question marks.

He heard the voice that seemed to come from the other side of the wall. "The three of us, we'll have a wonderful time."

Then he saw, beyond the curtain that showed all kinds of freakish possibilities, the living reality of Geraldine walking out of the kitchen. As he made a move to follow her, her hand flicked air, telling him to wait there. He told himself to wait, the woman had to go to the bathroom, and he sat down at the table and folded his fingers and stared at them and knew that his lips were trembling.

He heard the footsteps coming back to the kitchen, and turned to see Geraldine and the paper bag in her hand. She put the bag on the table, then reached in, and her fingers came out with a hypodermic syringe.

"Cocaine," she said. "In the trade they call it Charlie."

Chapter 18

H e tried to turn his eyes away from the plunger attached to the glass tube attached to the needle. But the thing told him he must keep on looking. And while that happened, Geraldine again reached into the paper bag and took out a little white box. She opened it and showed him the white capsules. There were three of them in there, three tiny entertainers in their jackets of shiny celluloid, singing in unison—come on in, the water's fine.

Geraldine added her voice to the chorus. "For a year now." She sounded very happy. "It's been a dandy, dandy year." Then the words went rolling down an incline. "A terrible year." She sounded sad. "Thought maybe I could stop and gave it a try. But what a laugh!" And after that, with the kind of frenzy that couldn't express itself in sound and showed only in the eyes, "Can't live without it, gotta have it, gotta have it."

He was trying to understand his reaction. There had been a moment of shock. But after that there was no astonishment, no dismay, no pity, and no disgust. Now, actually, he felt nothing at all beyond the blunt acknowledgment of the fact itself. Geraldine was a dope addict and her particular requirement was cocaine.

"Yes," she said, and sounded happy again. "I'm on it. Really on the junk. That's why I don't need much of that." She pointed to the icebox.

Then she pulled up her sleeve and showed him the upper part of her arm and he saw the marks of the needle.

"Get it?" she murmured. "I've really been to Arabia. Soon I'll be due for another trip. Or maybe it won't be Arabia. Maybe I'll be in the mood for Italy. A box seat in the Coliseum, right next to Nero, and watch the lions coming out. See the naked boys and girls running around,

166

trying to get away, and the lions just taking their own sweet time about it, moving in. Or sometimes I visit the hospitals, and drag them out of bed and open them up without giving them ether. You'd be amazed what sounds they can make."

He pointed to the capsules in the white box. "Isn't that expensive? Where do you get the money to buy it?"

"I push it," she said, then explained, "Bring in new customers. Not really what you'd call a pusher. All I do is hand out samples and pick up a commission when they really start to buy. There's a meeting once a week, and the board of directors gives me a list of what spots to hit."

"Like where?"

"Oh, anywhere. Certain taprooms. A house across the street from a high school. Anywhere." She picked up the white box and gazed adoringly at the capsules. "Damn right," she told them. "Damn right you're expensive. Two hundred dollars an ounce."

Then her eyes climbed very slowly from the capsules and she was looking appraisingly at Darby's eyes.

"Now listen," Darby said. "I don't want any part of this."

"Have I said anything?"

"No. And don't."

Her eyebrows went up above the dim smile. "What's all this all of a sudden?"

"Does it need an explanation? I just don't want any part of it, that's all."

"Well, all right, all right," she singsonged, in the manner of a gum-chewing chorus girl. She put the white box and the syringe in the paper bag and took the bag out of the room.

She came back to sit on his lap and put her arms around him. She leaned her head back to study his face and purred, "Mr. Alvin Darby."

It was like saying good-by to Mr. Alvin Darby and saying hello to a captive brought in wearing fetters.

A sort of stubborn captive who talked back now and then.

But it wouldn't take long to fix that.

"Come on," she whispered in his ear.

It was like being gradually devoured. But always it became the first time with someone unattainable but here anyway, here for just this one occasion and better make the most of it because the chance won't come again. But then later it was here again, saying, I want you. I want you.

For six days now he had been living here with Geraldine.

At Geraldine's instruction, he had written Vivian a letter with no return address on it. He had stated merely that matters had reached a point where he needed time to be alone and think things over, and he would be in touch with her as soon as he made up his mind. It was a vague sort of letter, and Geraldine said that was the way it should be. Just vague, not really saying anything definite. And yet just as emphatic as a smash on the skull with a sledge hammer.

After mailing the letter, he told Geraldine he doubted it would do the trick. Chances were, Vivian would call him at the office.

But Vivian did not call him at the office. There was no word at all from Vivian. And the office itself was nothing more than a technical eight hours a day wherein he earned the money that would fill the icebox up there in Kensington. Upon entering the office each morning he instantly became a machine that functioned with the required speed and precision to do the work and finish it and hand it in and get out. There were no more lunches with Harry Clawson. There was no contact at all with Harry. At first Harry had tried hard to re-establish contact, but received nothing more than silence and a blank stare. Then Harry became indignant and demanded to see the cards on the table and was quietly told to mind his own goddamn business. That more or less did it for Harry, who said, "All right, if that's the way you feel about it," and walked away and let it go at that.

So there in the office each day it was only the desk and the papers, the mathematics with the pencil checking the

logarithms, and the machine sitting there at the desk.
Until five o'clock.

After five o'clock he became a glowing-eyed animal in
a frantic hurry to get back to Kensington and the platinum-blonde hair.

Within these six days he had spent considerable cash.
To begin with, he mailed some money to Vivian. Then
he had to get some clothes because he had no intention
of going to that other house—his house. So he went out
and bought two suits and a dozen shirts and the rest of
the necessary haberdashery. And two pairs of shoes and
a razor and a hairbrush. But no pajamas. Geraldine rigidly rejected the idea of pajamas.

He bought Geraldine a jade bracelet she had seen in
a window. She said that was the only article she wanted
right now. He was sort of relieved that it was all she
wanted right now, because it was priced at $135 and it
brought the six-day expenditure up to the round sum of
three hundred dollars, leaving him a bank balance in the
round sum of eight hundred dollars.

So now it was the sixth day and he had come back from
work and was on the doorstep taking out the key that she
had given him. As he put it in the lock he heard his name
called and looked up to see Geraldine coming up the
street, the squirrel coat moving rapidly under the street
lamps rimmed with icicles and reflecting more light than
usual.

As she came nearer, he saw there was something wrong
with her face. It seemed that invisible pincers were working on her face and twisting it out of line. Her eyes were
a strange mixture of frenzy and fatigue, and the corners
of her lips were sagging, her mouth open and the breath
coming in short gasps.

She came up on the doorstep and didn't appear to know
he was there. Then he realized she actually didn't know
he was there. She reached toward the key and turned it,
opened the door, and lunged inside.

In the hall he grabbed her arm. "What's wrong?"

She tried to pull away.

"Tell me," he said. "You sick or something?"

She tightened her mouth, bent her head to one side to stare across the hall, and delivered him a vicious kick in the shin.

It didn't bother him much. He was sort of accustomed to it by now. In the six days there had been considerable kicking and scratching and throwing of plates and anything she could get her hands on.

What really bothered him was this strange condition of her face. He let go of her arm, took hold of her shoulders, and violently shook her until her head flopped loosely, like a doll's head with the spring broken.

"Goddamn you," he said. "Answer me."

She grinned at him. "You idiot." Then she grinned at the floor. "Can't you see I need a charge?"

He had never seen her when she needed the cocaine. He knew, of course, that she was taking the needle during the day, when he was at work. Since that one time when she had shown him the syringe and the capsules, there had been no talk about the cocaine. It was just an accepted fact between them that she used the stuff and handed out samples of it to get the money to keep on buying it. And that was all; there was no need on either side to discuss the matter further.

But now he saw the face of Geraldine when she really needed it, and it was like looking at a mask made of dead skin painted yellow-white.

And he heard the cackling sound that seemed to come from the eyes instead of the lips.

"Charlie," she cackled. "I need Charlie."

"Good God," he said aloud to himself, and stepped back and saw her moving down the dark hall, a monster squirrel walking on its hind legs. Because he didn't see the hands and he didn't see the ankles. He didn't even see the platinum-blonde hair. There wasn't enough light, and all he saw was the gray shape walking away and down through the darkness.

Until he saw the light go on in the bedroom.

Then she called to him in a loud cackle, "Come on in. Come in, Alvin dear, and I'll let you watch."

He turned and stared at the front door. It was still

open. He moved toward it, with no other intention than the idea of closing it to keep out the cold wind. But as he put his hand on the knob he realized the meaning of the door. It was still open. There was nothing to prevent him from walking out.

He heard Geraldine calling, "What's the delay? Come on in. You'll see something nice."

He closed the door and turned and walked down the hall to the bedroom. He saw Geraldine hunched over on the edge of the bed, the arms out of the sleeves and the upper part of the dress rolled down to the waist. In one hand she had the syringe and two fingers of the other hand squeezed the flesh of the arm dotted with needle marks. She transferred the syringe from one hand to the other, sat up straight, and began to breathe the way a fighter breathes between rounds. Then she gazed with rapture at the needle and inserted it into the vein and pressed the plunger that slowly lowered the level of cocaine in the glass tube.

Then the tube was empty and the syringe sort of glided out and away from her fingers. She was flat on her back on the bed, still breathing very hard, her mouth wide open. Her eyes looked straight at Darby and saw a medium-sized man with hazel eyes and straw-colored hair, wearing a raglan coat that now began to dissolve into nothing more than a rag around the waist of an otherwise naked creature chained to a pillar of stone, while she. instructed the attendants to open the cage that held the two starved hyenas. Then her eyes were the two hyenas coming out of the cage and running lightly toward the feast.

Darby backed out of the room and closed the door. He went into the kitchen and put a light under the coffee. He put a cigarette in his mouth and struck a match, then moved toward the window and looked out. There wasn't much of a view; the window was screened with frost. But he could see the lights of houses on the other side of the alley, and flickering shapes of women moving back and forth in kitchens. In actual distance the people in those other houses were maybe twenty, thirty feet away. But it

was like seeing them through a telescope on another
planet, just about able to see them, never able to reach
them.

Never again.

And suddenly he was very tired. He sat down at the
table, lowered his head into his arms, and went sliding
down a tunnel of sleep.

Many hours later he was awakened by the hand gripping and shaking his shoulder.

He raised his head from the table and looked up and
saw Geraldine and heard her saying, "Come on."

"Where?"

"To bed."

She was wearing the squirrel coat. It was unbuttoned.
There was nothing underneath.

He followed Geraldine into the bedroom. She took
off the squirrel coat to stand there naked with her back
to the orange face of the electric heater. She shimmied just
a little as she let the glowing wires warm her spine. The
heater was on a low table next to the bed, and after some
moments she sat on the edge of the bed and let the heater
warm her legs.

Darby leaned sideways against the door, watching the
naked body of Geraldine moving this way, that way,
drinking in the orange glimmer of the electric heater.

He saw flecks of bright orange dancing on the pools of
the pale green eyes, and the breasts thrusting up to get
sprayed with the orange glow.

She was grinning at him and murmuring, "Don't get
undressed yet. I'll tell you when to get undressed. Right
now I want to talk to you."

Then she reached backward across the bed, her fingers
playing idly with the little white box. She placed the box
on her lap and opened it and he saw it contained a single
capsule.

She grinned down at the capsule and said, "It gets
monotonous when you work for other people. Especially
when all you do is hand out samples. I've brought in I
don't know how many customers, and I'm still waiting to
see some decent money."

Her voice was going up and down, as though she were singing a song that had no special tune. Every few moments her shoulders twitched, as if she were trying to shake off a fly.

The shoulders twitched and the head gave a little jump to send the eyes darting toward a man who was too quiet. It ought to be Arabia, a stone cellar, there ought to be a white-hot poker in her hand, and maybe then he wouldn't be so quiet. Oh, no, he wouldn't be quiet then.

She grinned at the floor. "I want some of that decent money." She pulled a lever that shut off the grin as she looked at Darby. "I'm going into business for myself."

He pointed to the white box. "Selling that?"

She snorted. "No. Selling airplanes." Then she raised her eyebrows. "Say, that isn't bad, you know? I'll be in the airplane business. Taking my customers off the ground."

"You'll wind up getting—"

"Shut up," she cut in. "Don't tell the boss how to run the business. All you'll do is work for the boss." She stretched her arm rigid to point her finger at him. "Starting tomorrow I'm putting you to work."

It came at him too fast and he didn't know what to say.

Geraldine crossed her legs and lifted her hand to appraise the orange luster on her fingernails. She said, "How much you got in the bank?"

"Now listen—"

"How much?" she said softly. "How much, Alvin?"

"Eight hundred."

"Good."

"Now wait. Listen—"

"Tomorrow you take it out. Every cent of it. You hear me?" She got up off the bed and came toward him. She took hold of his wrist and patted his hand. "We'll make a lot of money, Alvin."

He pulled his hand away. "Not me. Don't count me in."

As though he hadn't spoken, she said, "I know the trade. All the angles. I got the right connections, too. Know when the boats come in and who to see on the boats. And I can take it off the boat at, say, around a hundred and ten an ounce."

He gazed past her. "I don't know what you're talking about. I'm in the insurance business."

"Not any more." Then again she had hold of his wrist and was patting his hand. "Take a look at this layout. We start with the eight hundred and it buys close to eight ounces. We sell at the market price, two hundred. At the very least we'll sell ten, twelve ounces a week."

He shook his head.

"Don't do that," Geraldine said.

He went on shaking his head.

"I said don't do that." She swung her arm and banged the back of her hand against his face. "I don't like it when you do that." She hit him again. "Don't ever do that." She reached up to take hold of his hair to hold him still while she banged his face. "Tomorrow," hitting him, "you bring me," hitting him, "the eight," hitting him, "hundred," hitting him, "dollars."

He stood there and took it. All the spine and the spirit went away and it was just the shell of the man standing there and taking it.

"You stupid square," she screeched. "You obstinate fool, you ever say no to me again and I'll cripple you." She turned away from him, went to the bed, and picked up the white box. She took the capsule out of the box and came back to him and held the capsule in front of his eyes. "You see this? This is Charlie."

He stared at the capsule. The hunger was a seed that suddenly flowered.

Geraldine said, "You want it, don't you?"

He went on staring at Charlie.

"Sure you do," Geraldine said. "You really need it. I can tell."

Then she threw her head back and he heard the cackling laughter, but now it didn't bother him at all.

"Well," she laughed. "Well, whaddya know?" She talked to the capsule. "He wants you, Charlie. He really does. And that makes it just fine. Now he's a member." She looked at Darby. "Aren't you?"

He nodded.

"Wonderful," she said. And then, to the capsule, "But

we knew, didn't we? We knew all along. He was bound to come in." She gave Darby a pat on the shoulder. "Good boy." She grinned. "You'll be a dandy salesman. When you use it yourself, the sales talk comes easy."

She reached over to the bed and picked up the hypodermic syringe and let the capsule caress the glass tube.

She murmured, "I might as well tell you, it'll hurt like hell. It's a lot easier when you sniff it up your nose, or take it like a pill. Especially when you take it for the first time. But I'll leave that up to you. How do you want it?"

"The needle," he said.

She frowned just a little. "You want it to hurt, don't you?"

He didn't say anything.

So all she did then was shrug, and her head turned and her eyes swept the room, searching for something. "Guess it isn't here," she mumbled. And louder, "Well, there's more in the bathroom. You'll find it in the medicine cabinet. A roll of cotton."

He went into the bathroom and opened the medicine cabinet and reached toward the blue paper package of absorbent cotton. But before he could touch it, his eyes shifted to the top shelf.

They focused on a little brown bottle labeled "Iodine." With the warning in thick letters, "Poison."

Perhaps it was a better friend than Charlie.

His hand moved toward the little brown bottle.

Chapter 19

JUST THEN HE HEARD the grinding voice that came from the bedroom: "What the hell are you doing in there?"

He didn't reply. His fingers circled the little brown bottle.

The bathroom door was open and he heard the abrupt approach of her footsteps. Well it would only take a second. He'd be able to do it before she could stop him.

He had the bottle in his hand and he was pulling at the rubber cap. But suddenly his eyes aimed at something else, and he put the little brown bottle back in the medicine cabinet. He went on staring at the larger bottle on the lower shelf. A bottle labeled "Peroxide."

Peroxide, the stuff the girls used to change the color of their hair from dark to blonde and then to platinum blonde. From dark to platinum blonde . . .

Slowly he closed the cabinet door and his eyes bored into the mirror. And the eyes in the mirror were Marjorie's eyes, and they snapped with excitement and defiance beneath the silvery hair. Her lips did not move, but he could hear her voice, coming from a great distance and growing louder: "Yes, I bleached it. Why shouldn't I? I like it. I'm nearly sixteen now, and I guess I can bleach my hair if I want to."

He turned slowly and saw her standing there, saw the pale green eyes and the silver-yellow hair glimmering. Standing there, so radiant and wonderful.

The sweetest and the nicest. And he was her best boy friend.

His smile was tender. "You're so pretty," he said. "You're the prettiest girl I've ever seen."

Geraldine frowned. "What goes on here?"

"I mean it," he said. "You're like a princess."

176

Geraldine put a hand on her hip and slanted her head. "What's the play? What are you giving me?"

"I like you so much. So very much. Up to the sky and down again."

"Well, thanks, kiddo," she said, the frown playing tag with a smile as she stood there trying to figure it out. "You say it like you're really serious."

He nodded solemnly. "I'd do anything for you. Anything."

He looked up. And it wasn't the ceiling of the bathroom, it was the dark and lustrous sky above Fairmount Park, and he could see the moon.

"What are you looking at?" Geraldine asked.

"The moon."

"Say," she murmured, "that's frantic talk. That really sends me."

He moved toward her. Very gently he put his arms around her and touched his lips to her forehead.

And he said, "I'm so happy when I'm near you. It's all I want. When I'm near you I don't care about anything else."

The tenderness pleased her and puzzled her and she closed her eyes and told herself it was something new. She had heard a lot about this thing called tenderness, but not once in all her life had it entered her experience. Now that it was happening, she decided she liked it.

She took his hand and led him down the hall, toward the bedroom.

And it wasn't the hall and they weren't going toward a bedroom. They were walking across the grass, toward the bushes.

Then, in the bedroom, Geraldine put out the light. She told herself she wasn't in the mood for the bright light and the mirror. She didn't even feel like using the kind of language she usually used when they were in the bed together.

He sat beside her on the edge of the bed.

It was so dark and quiet here in the bushes, with the moonlight coming through, the soft blue glow. And the perfume of the violets. And the kind of delight that couldn't be measured, there was so much of it. Just because he was here with her and they were alone together.

"Let's always stay here," he breathed. "Let's never leave this place."

Geraldine wanted to say that she was fed up with Kensington and as soon as they had enough cabbage in the pot they'd get a fancy apartment downtown. But somehow she couldn't say it. Somehow it didn't quite fit in with what was happening.

She said, "You really go for me, don't you?"

"I think of you all the time," he whispered. "All day long I keep seeing you. I can't wait until school lets out."

"School lets out." She repeated the phrase as though experimenting with it. "That sounds nice. That's really nice, I dig that."

He held her hand. "Make me a promise."

"Sure. What is it?"

"Promise you'll never go away."

She wanted to laugh. It was really funny. Of course she'd never go away. Where the hell could she go?

But then, in a way, it wasn't funny at all, as she checked the item that couldn't be ignored at this particular moment. It was the fact that she just couldn't stay with one man for much longer than it took to get him wrapped up and neatly tied in the palm of her hand. Sooner or later she'd be sick and tired of this one. If he got too attached to her, she might have trouble getting rid of him. Maybe worse than the trouble of a couple years back, when some big bastard whose name she didn't remember had beat her up so bad they had to take her to a hospital.

Well, there was no point in worrying about it. Worry about it later, when the time came.

She leaned her head against his shoulder and said, "I give you my sacred word, I'll never go away."

And so then he turned and put his arms around her. He kissed the lips and tasted the nectar of her treasured mouth. His eyes were closed and he felt the warm shiver running through him as Marjorie hugged him close. The warmth increased and became a hotness that made him sort of afraid because it was getting hotter and hotter and all at once it was a flame and he couldn't do anything to stop it. Marjorie was breathing hard and she was taking off her shoes and doing something with her hands underneath her skirt, like adjusting something, or loosening something. Just watching her doing that caused the flame inside him to burn so hot that it felt as though he were burning up. And then, there in the bushes, with the moon and the violets and all, he was crazily eager and he was terribly afraid. He wondered what Marjorie expected him to do. He tried to say something but the words got all mixed up in his throat as Marjorie seemed to come closer and closer even though she was flat on her back and not moving at all. She was moaning and sighing and all at once he wondered what he was doing to her because she let out a smothered cry and said, "Don't, don't, don't."

But he couldn't do anything to stop the flame. It burned and burned and then it exploded and Marjorie cried out again, louder.

There was a moment of nothing and he wondered what he had done.

The moment became a hatchet, chopping away at him, as he realized what he had done.

On tracks of rapid transit he made the return trip from then to now, seeing the reason of it all. For the nightmare of guilt. For the hidden torment. And he told himself he had served enough time in the prison of his brain. And so the guilt of his youth came into the light, exposed before him, and he saw it clear and full before it vanished, faded away for all time. Some thirty minutes later Geraldine was sitting on the edge of the bed and staring at him as he buttoned the collar of his shirt. Then he reached for the necktie and Geraldine leaned back on her elbows and frowned puzzledly.

He bent toward the dresser mirror and slipped the necktie around the collar and began working it into a knot.

Geraldine said, "Just where do you think you're going?"

"I've already told you," he murmured, concentrating on the necktie. "I'm clearing out."

He finished with the necktie and picked up his jacket.
"Put that down," Geraldine said.

He just stood there and smiled at her.

She got up off the bed and took a step toward him.
"Put it down," she commanded. "Damn you, do as I
say."

"Don't be a fool," he said mildly.

She studied his eyes. For a moment her lips were tight.
Then all at once she sighed resignedly and relaxed
against the wall and grinned at the man who was now
just another casual acquaintance.

"What did it?" she asked. "What broke up the party?"

He didn't answer. He was putting his arms through
the sleeves of the raglan.

"I'm really curious," Geraldine said. "Just a little
while ago you were so tender. So sweet and affectionate."
She went on grinning at him, "What the hell was all
that about?"

He was slowly buttoning the raglan. "I wasn't saying
those things to you. I was talking to someone else."

Geraldine shrugged. "Well, anyway," she said, "it
sounded nice." And then, "Come on, I'll walk you to the
door." She slipped into a robe.

They went out of the bedroom and down the hall to
the front door. He looked out through the door window
and saw the Plymouth parked on the other side of the
street.

He started to open the door, and heard Geraldine saying, "Where will you go now?"

"Home," he said. "I'm going back to my wife."

"How do you know she'll be there?"

"She'll be there." He opened the door wider.

Geraldine moved back from the door to get away from
the cold air. She smiled at him and said, "Well, so
long."

"Good-by, Geraldine."

He walked out and closed the door and started across
the pavement. But something caused him to turn and
look back. And through the door window he saw the
dark hallway in there and a thing that glowed in the

darkness. It was the platinum-blonde hair, going away. Going farther and farther away and gradually drowning in the shadows.

THE END

Also by David Goodis and published by Serpent's Tail

The Blonde on the Street Corner

She took a final drag at the cigarette, flipped it away, and said, "I don't get this line of talk. It's way over my head. I think you have been reading fairy-tales, or something. Maybe you're waiting for some dream girl to come along in a coach drawn by six white horses, and she'll pick you up and haul you away to the clouds, where it's all milk and honey and springtime all year around. Maybe that's what you're waiting for. That dream girl."

"Maybe," he murmured. And then he looked at the blonde. His smile was soft and friendly and he said, "I guess that's why I can't start with you. I'm waiting for the dream girl."

But the dream girl does not come. In the meantime Ralph must deal with the yearnings of everyday life and take what he is offered.

Written in 1954, *The Blonde on the Street Corner* is full of the passions and desires that are the hallmarks of a David Goodis novel.

"His books are a lethally potent cocktail of surreal description, brilliant language, cracker barrel philosophy and gripping obsession" Adrian Wootton

The Moon in the Gutter

Introduction by Adrian Wootton

In a back street in the rough end of Philadelphia, docker William Kerrigan obsesses over the mysterious suicide of his sister. Into a dive bar walks Loretta Channing the beautiful, enigmatic socialite and sister of Newton the drunk. For Kerrigan, Loretta's the impossible dream, the escape route out of his hellhole existence, away from the crowded tenements, the shacks, the dark alleys. But Loretta may also hold the key to finding out what prompted his sister's death, the reason he can never break free.

The Moon in the Gutter is a fierce and heated tale of desire and revenge. Made into a film starring Gerard Depardieu and Nastassia Kinski, it remains an enthralling classic of American noir fiction.